The Priscilla Diary

The
Priscilla
DIARY
GENE EDWARDS

Tyndale House Publishers, Inc.
Wheaton, Illinois

Visit Tyndale's exciting Web site at www.tyndale.com

The Priscilla Diary

Edited by MaryLynn Layman

Scripture quotations are taken from the *Holy Bible*, New Living Translation, copyright © 1996. Used by permission of Tyndale House Publishers, Inc., Wheaton, Illinois 60189. All rights reserved.

Library of Congress Cataloging-in-Publication Data

Edwards, Gene
   The Priscilla diary / Gene Edwards.
     p. cm — (First century diaries)
   ISBN 0-8423-3870-5 (sc)
     1. Paul, the Apostle, Saint—Fiction. 2. Priscilla, Saint,
1st cent.—Fiction. 3. Church History—Primitive and early
church, ca. 30-600—Fiction. 4. Rome—History—Empire,
30 B.C.-284 A.D.—Fiction. 5. Christian women saints—Fiction.
6. Corinth (Greece)—Fiction. I. Title

   PS3555.D924 P75 2001
   813'.54—dc21   00-053204

Printed in the United States of America

08 07 06 05 04 03 02 01
7   6   5   4   3   2   1

Dedicated to Pam Spires and Mary Santo, Kathy McGraw, Alison Booth, and Jenny Jeffries—each has been a Priscilla in my life and ministry.

BOOKS BY **GENE EDWARDS**

First-Century Diaries
The Silas Diary
The Titus Diary
The Timothy Diary
The Priscilla Diary
*The Gaius Diary**

The Chronicles of the Door
The Beginning
The Escape
The Birth
The Triumph
The Return

In a Class by Themselves
The Divine Romance
Revolutionary Bible Study

The Deeper Christian Life
The Highest Life
The Secret to the Christian Life
The Inward Journey

Comfort and Healing for the Inner Man
Crucified by Christians
Letters to a Devastated Christian
Dear Lilian
The Prisoner in the Third Cell
A Tale of Three Kings

Church Life/House Church
How to Meet in Homes
Revolution: The Story of the Early Church
Climb the Highest Mountain
When the Church Was Led Only by Laymen
An Open Letter to House Church Leaders
Overlooked Christianity

*Coming soon

PROLOGUE

I have just received word that Timothy is dead.

Of the original Twelve, only John is left. I have aged along-side Paul and his coworkers, and, one by one, I have seen all die except Gaius. Paul met his end in Rome. Barnabas gave up his spirit on his beloved island of Cyprus. Silas went to be with his Lord when the Roman sword took his life on the Greek island of Rhodes.

Of the eight men Paul trained in Ephesus, Aristarchus was the first to die. Secundus died at the hands of Nero, as did Sopater. Titus was crucified on the island of Crete, where he had been faithfully serving his Lord. Now our beloved Timothy's life has come to an end in the city of Ephesus. Of the Eight, only Gaius is alive.

You have read of Paul and Barnabas's first journey, as chronicled by Silas. You have read of Paul's second journey, as told by Titus. Then Timothy recorded the remarkable story of Paul and the eight men he trained in Ephesus.

Some time later Timothy wrote to me, Priscilla, and asked that I continue the story, taking up at the point where a riot broke out in Ephesus. Timothy's request of me will be no easy task. Nonetheless, now that Timothy is dead, I am determined to carry out his request.

There is so much to tell: Paul's trip to Dalmatia, the riot in Jerusalem, Paul's imprisonment in Caesarea, and his effort to reach Rome. What an abundance of events took place in so short a time.

When Aquila and I first met Paul in Corinth, I was in my early twenties. Today I am quite old. (You might say that I am ancient!) When I look back on all those wonder-filled years, I feel they happened but yesterday. And as I reflect, yes, I find that I desire to tell you everything that happened after that riot in Ephesus.

Let us, therefore, return to Ephesus and to the uprising that so abruptly ended Paul's time there.

Paul had been in Ephesus three years, raising up a church *and* eight young workers. I must tell you, these eight men became marvelous men indeed!

I will begin by telling you of the riot in Ephesus. When it began it had all the makings of a tragedy, but it ended much more like a comedy!

CHAPTER 1

Twenty-four thousand men screaming at the top of their lungs as they rushed through the streets of Ephesus, crying out *"Megale he Artemis Ephesian!"* is a sight not to be forgotten. It was the greatest riot in the five hundred-year history of the city, and it all had to do with Paul!

Alas, Paul did have ways of getting into trouble—none more than that spring day in Ephesus.

I have often been asked, "Were you there when the riot happened?" Yes, I was there; however, being a woman, I was not in the amphitheater. I missed seeing over twenty thousand men foolishly shouting . . . about *what* I did not know! Neither did they!

This riot occurred during the Games of Artemis. (These games are held once every two years in Ephesus.) This is a time when people from all over the empire come to watch great athletes from dozens of nations pit themselves against one another.

What started the riot? Even to this day, no one really knows. Early one morning, though, just about the time the games were getting underway, the guild of the silversmiths met together near the city theater. The meeting was led by

Demetrius, the largest seller of silver in Asia Minor. It was a grim meeting. The previous twelve months had been bad for sales of idols. All present knew why. Hundreds of magicians and tricksters had burned their books of dark magic in a bonfire in the marketplace! The people of Ephesus, as well as visitors, had stopped buying these men's idols in large numbers as they had in previous years. Many local magicians, as well as the ordinary citizens of Ephesus, had turned away from superstitions—all because of words spoken by Paul.

As Timothy reported in his diary, "When anyone in the market asked Paul about magic, he denounced it. And then he denounced all the magicians in the city. 'They are frauds,' he declared. Paul's words came to receptive ears, for deep in their hearts most everyone in the city already knew that. Nonetheless, they managed both to see the magicians as frauds and at the same time depend on them."

Now that the games had begun, would sales continue to fall? *This* was the central topic of the guild.

But why the riot?

By tradition, on the opening day of the games, a huge procession of people march from the Temple of Artemis down to the city's north gate. The procession then enters the city by way of Marble Street, which is just at the base of the theater, and winds its way up the hill, then past the city hall. From there the procession passes out of the city through the Magnesia gate, where the parade ends.

The guild was meeting near the main entranceway to the great amphitheater, which is located on Market Street, at the center of the city.

The members of the guild were becoming rowdy and belligerent, a result of hearing a highly inflammatory speech made by Demetrius. Here is that speech. You might say that this is the source of the riot:

Gentlemen, you know that our wealth comes from this business. As you have seen and heard, this man Paul has persuaded many people that handmade gods aren't gods at all. And this is happening not only here in Ephesus but throughout the entire province! Of course, I'm not just talking about the loss of public respect for our business. I'm also concerned that the temple of the great goddess Artemis will lose its influence and that Artemis—this magnificent goddess worshiped throughout the province of Asia and all around the world—will be robbed of her prestige!

When the speech ended, the agitated silversmiths moved into the streets crying out: "Great is Artemis of the Ephesians!"

Those in the parade joined in shouting the chant. Some onlookers thought this was the signal for the beginning of some athletic contest inside the theater. In good humor, they joined in the chant *and* moved into the amphitheater. But the silversmiths were not in a kind state of mind. Someone among them called out: "Let us bring the troublemaker here! He should be easy to find; he is always either in the market or at the school of Tyrannus."

Several in the guild rushed through the streets crying, "Where is Paul of Tarsus?"

Then began the confusion. Some thought these silversmiths were chasing a robber. Others thought the city fathers had called a special meeting in the theater. (Such assemblies always began with the chant, "Great is Artemis of the Ephesians.") Hearing the clamor, people in the marketplace, out of curiosity, followed those entering the theater. What everyone saw was men rushing toward the theater. In the theater, the chanting grew louder.

Those who ran to the school of Tyrannus looking for Paul found only Tyrannus. He was giving his morning lecture on the teachings of Plato. But their search for Paul was not wholly in vain. They found Gaius of Derbe and Aristarchus of Thessalonica. The two men were summarily dragged through the streets toward the theater. By now those in the market-place—crowded with visitors—were certain something extraordinary was taking place. Hearing the chant "Great is Artemis of the Ephesians!" and seeing men being dragged through the streets heightened their curiosity. Who could resist the mystery? (Further, Gaius's loud protest only fueled that curiosity.)

Soon the entire marketplace, for absolutely no reason, took up the chant. The chant, in turn, echoed out across the city. The crowd grew in number. By now Aristarchus and Gaius had been dragged into the theater and up onto the stage. Gaius, kicking and screaming, had to be lifted off his feet and carried onto the stage.

"Enemies of Artemis are here!" someone shouted. And so the senseless chant grew even louder. That did it. Almost every man in Ephesus was soon on his way to the center of the city.

Regardless of who entered the theater, each took up the chant. Most were smiling. After all, Gaius was providing quite a show.

I might mention that at that particular time the theater was still under construction, not to be finished until the same year as the destruction of Jerusalem. Slaves who had been working at the construction site ran in terror.

The theater had been carved out of the side of a hill. The top entrance provided one with a view that stretched from Ephesus out to the glistening Aegean Sea.

The acoustics within the amphitheater were excellent, and the chant was reverberating across the city and out into the countryside. By now men were closing up their shops, farmers were leaving their fields, and the marketplace was vacant as men ran toward the amphitheater. Homes, too, began to empty. As far out as the port, men were rushing toward the amphitheater, all taking up the chant.

It was a sight to see *and* hear. Women and children were asking what the noise was all about. No clear answer was forthcoming. The only thing most people really knew was that their local goddess was receiving a very loud chant! (This disturbance marked the very first time the unfinished theater was filled.)

The confusing incident was fast becoming a comedy! When Timothy discovered that the whole episode had to do with Paul, he muttered, "Oh no! A *crowd*. If Paul hears there is a crowd, he will try to speak to it!" With that Timothy set out in a fury to find Secundus. (The other brothers were out in the towns and cities around Ephesus preaching to the young churches they had recently raised up.)

Once Timothy located Secundus he said, "Secundus, there is some sort of a melee, a huge crowd, in the theater. Help me find Paul. When you do, sit on him if you must, but do not let him get near the theater. Send for others to help you. It may take all of us to stop Paul, but whatever it takes, do not let Paul go inside that theater!"

Secundus understood immediately. He set out for the port, as he had heard Paul might be there.

Because of Timothy's efforts, a dozen brothers were soon scurrying through the streets desperately trying to find someone who knew *exactly* where Paul was. Having at last found him at the harbor, they discovered he was oblivious to the fact there was a riot going on in the city. Like many others, Paul thought the commotion had to do with the games.

True to his ways, when Paul heard that Gaius and Aristarchus had been dragged into the amphitheater, that a large crowd had assembled, and that he himself was the center of the disturbance, Paul determined to enter the theater and address the crowd. Whether or not the young men could have prevented him we will never know. It was my dear husband, Aquila, who stopped Paul. Aquila is a very quiet man. He rarely offers an opinion, and when he speaks, men listen—*even* Paul! Aquila stepped right in front of Paul, looked him straight in the eye and said: "You will not go into the theater." That is all Aquila said.

Paul tensed, then relaxed, not uttering a single word as a rejoinder. Paul knew, as did the other men, that if Aquila felt that strongly, even Paul would yield to his words.

While this hidden scene was going on, yet another scene was unfolding at the Jewish synagogue.

Alexander, one of the Jewish leaders, heard that the theater was filled with men screaming their allegiance to Artemis and that Paul was the cause of the commotion. Alexander decided to go to the theater and address the throng, with the view that he would let the men of Ephesus know that the local Jews, particularly the ones of the synagogue, were *not* followers of Paul. Alexander had misjudged the hour. He saw this as a perfect time to let the entire city know that Paul was a foreign Jew and a renegade. It was not to be so.

When Alexander entered the theater, he immediately stepped onto the stage and raised one hand for silence. The crowd exploded! They instantly recognized his Hebrew dress. And Hebrews did *not* worship Artemis. The chant turned into a threatening scream. Alexander and those with him made a hasty retreat. The chant rolled on.

I was by then standing just outside the theater, hoping to hear some word of the fate of Gaius and Aristarchus. The ground was literally shaking under my feet. I feared for the lives of both our dear brothers.

At last, word of the demonstration reached the ears of the *asiarch*, or mayor. He was, at that moment, at the temple. The asiarch had already sent a messenger to find out what the unscheduled assembly was about, but as the thunderous roll of men's voices increased, he decided not to wait for a reply.

By the time he reached the theater the asiarch had some vague idea of what had provoked this unseemly outburst. He paused, took a deep breath, and stepped onto the stage. He was immediately recognized and then was met with an ovation of approval. He raised his hand; the assembly fell silent. He then uttered words that every man in the stadium fully understood.

> Should the Romans hear about this riot, Ephesus could very well be run over with armed Roman soldiers. Worse, our freedom could even be taken away from us.

As I reflect on this event, I now realize that it was no small mercy that the arch asiarch was Paul's friend!) Luke was in the stadium watching the entire incident. Later Luke chronicled the asiarch's words:

> At last the mayor was able to quiet them down enough to speak. "Citizens of Ephesus," he said. "Everyone knows that Ephesus is the official guardian of the temple of the great Artemis, whose image fell down to us from heaven. Since this is an indisputable fact, you shouldn't be disturbed, no matter what is said. Don't do anything rash. You have brought these men here, but they have stolen nothing from the temple and have not spoken against our goddess. If Demetrius and the craftsmen have a case against them, the courts are in session and the judges can take the case at once. Let them go through legal channels. And if there are complaints about other matters, they can be settled in a legal assembly. I am afraid we are in danger of being charged with rioting by the Roman government, since there is no cause for all this commotion. And if Rome demands an explanation, we won't know what to say."

The asiarch then proceeded to dismiss the assembly. The stadium emptied almost instantly.

"You two—are you well enough to return to your home?" the asiarch asked of Aristarchus and Gaius.

"I am not," replied Gaius, trying to imitate Paul's bravado after being beaten and imprisoned in Philippi.

"Whatever your condition, if you can walk, I urge you to leave!"

Aristarchus whispered to Gaius: "Let us go quickly. You are *not* a Roman citizen, and I see no evidence that you are about to receive an apology."

Gaius, cut, bleeding, and seriously injured, managed to hobble to my home.

In the meantime, Paul knew instinctively that he was spending his last hours in Ephesus. That night all the believers in Ephesus came together in one place to hear Paul's last words and to bid him farewell.

CHAPTER 2

I had already planned to depart Ephesus in a few days, my destination Corinth. For quite some time I have been planning to be in Corinth at the time of the festival of Pentecost. I have already written to them informing them of my plans. I would have already left for Corinth except that the Games of Artemis presented me with a wide door of opportunity. This is one reason that I delayed my departure. As you know, because of this delay I sent Titus to Corinth in my place.

"Today, the riot has changed my plans yet again. Obviously I will not be here during the games."

Everyone laughed.

"Perhaps the Lord favored your original plans," someone called out.

"I tend to agree," replied Paul. "My point is this: I must leave now, but keep in mind I would have left in a few days anyway.

"This very morning I was at the port inquiring of a ship bound for Troas. Titus is to come from Corinth and meet me in Troas a few days from now. Hopefully, he will bring good news of the assembly in Corinth. My earlier letter to Corinth was very strong. By now, the crisis in the church in Corinth has either abated or become worse.

"To say the least, I am anxious to hear from Titus. My hope is that the word from Corinth will be good. However," (I can still see Paul's eyes twinkle) "you can never know about those Greeks. They are not nice, quiet, peace-loving people like the Ephesians!"

After the laughter died down, Paul continued: "If I do not find Titus at Troas, we have both agreed that I will meet him in Philippi, Greece. After I see Titus, I hope to return to you!"

At this everyone applauded and cheered.

"By the time I return to you, I trust that most of the people in this city will have forgotten Paul of Tarsus and his friends."

"But *we* will never forget *them*," groaned Gaius.

"I promised eight young men that I would take them to Jerusalem. Therefore, after I return to you, we will sail to Israel, disembarking at Caesarea-by-the-Sea, and then . . . Jerusalem," Paul said and then paused.

"One last word. Right now, a number of brothers and sisters from Gentile churches are leaving their homes and going to Rome . . . at my request. I have asked all of them not to go directly to Rome but rather to gather at Philippi and from Philippi to all go together to Rome."

"How many, Paul?"

"About forty believers. I will see them all in Philippi."

A flurry of questions ensued. Then all eyes turned toward my husband and me.

"Priscilla," Paul said motioning to me. "Tell us of *your* plans. Tell the brothers and sisters how *you* plan to reach Rome."

I replied, "Aquila, Epenetus, and I will also leave Ephesus in a few days, and go straight to Philippi. From there the three of us go to Rome. I estimate it will take another three months for all forty of the Gentile believers to reach Philippi, but we three plan to be in Philippi for only a few days. I need to be in Rome before all those people arrive."

"Priscilla plans to reach Rome, settle into her new house, *and* be ready to receive an overenthusiastic group of forty Gentiles who are coming from all over the empire. Now *that* is my wife!" Aquila announced.

"The house I bought needs very little attention," I explained. "Right now, friends of mine in Rome are furnishing the house for us. We will need very little time to receive our many sojourners. I only hope there will be *more* than forty who come!"

"So, dear Ephesians," said Paul. "Tomorrow I leave for Troas along with Luke and seven others. Then in just a few days Priscilla, Aquila, and Epenetus will also be leaving you."

There was a long silence. Then my husband spoke again. "We found that there is a ship scheduled to sail from here straight to Greece, that is, to Philippi. That ship arrived here *today*—on the day of the riot!"

Again, everyone cheered.

"It is a grain ship, but it is taking passengers. They plan to sail for Philippi in about seven days."

The believers, as one, leapt to their feet and surrounded us. It was for me an unforgettable moment. My husband and I had been in Ephesus for four years. When we arrived, not one person in that room was a believer. Now we watched with joy as hundreds gathered around us, touched us, called out to us, and then sang to us and prayed for us.

The meeting ended with tears . . . and joy.

Paul's journey north to Troas would be very brief.

Dawn came soon. Paul stood on the piers of Ephesus sharing a few last words. He said, "If I see Titus in Troas, I will stay in Troas for a few days to proclaim Christ there. Oddly, the situation in Troas is unique. My sworn enemy, who follows me wherever I go, has been to the synagogue in Troas. He even met with its leaders, yet without success. The Jews in Troas still like me! I see an open door in Troas.

"If Titus is not there I will go immediately to Philippi, hoping Priscilla and Aquila will have arrived there by then. And if God pleases, I will not only see Titus, but I hope to also watch Priscilla and Aquila board a ship for Rome. Further, God willing, in about a year, I shall join them in Rome.

"Right now I cannot but make this voyage alone, for all the men I have trained are here. Trophimus, Secundus, and Tychicus are in the countryside. It will take several days to find them. After they get back to Ephesus they will go straight to Philippi. I will go to Troas alone.

There was a prayer and a final farewell. Little did we know that Paul was about to be plunged into the darkest days of his entire life.

CHAPTER 3

Paul motioned to Aquila, Luke, and Timothy to go on board with him briefly. He confided:

"I am pressed out of measure concerning the body of Christ in Corinth. There are times that I fear the gathering there no longer exists. I have had many sleepless nights over the church there. Nevertheless, something else weighs just as heavily upon me. I am distraught concerning the safety of Titus. Because of the Daggermen, just being my coworker is a threat to Titus's life. Only once before have I ever felt so desperate; it was on the way to Thessalonica from Philippi on my first visit to that land. Timothy, you remember I had just learned that Blastinius had made a vow to destroy every church I raised up." (That journey from Philippi to Thessalonica had marked the lowest point in Paul's life. Now he had come again to such a dark hour.)

Aquila, Luke, and Timothy hugged Paul, bid him farewell, and hurried off the boat.

Soon after Paul finished confiding his heart and his dear friends left, the weather began to turn inclement. Shortly, the ship, like Paul, was being tossed about by stormy seas. Being alone did not help.

Seven days later, Aquila, Epenetus, Luke, and I sailed for Philippi, every moment asking ourselves: "Will Paul find Titus when he reaches Troas?" We would know the answer to that question on the very day we reached Philippi. But what if Titus had not arrived in Philippi? None of us wanted to consider that possibility. The reason was simple. If Titus never reached Philippi or Troas . . . he might be dead!

When we arrived in Philippi, Lydia was there to meet us. As Paul had often told me, she was one of the dearest of all the saints. But, on that day, I could remember only one sentence she spoke:

"No, Titus has not arrived in Philippi. Worse, word has reached us that the Daggermen have killed someone in Corinth. Whether the rumor be true or not, we do not know."

Instantly we knew that Paul, upon reaching Troas, would not find Titus. He would be a distraught, desperate man, not only facing the possible loss of the gathering in Corinth, but also the possible loss of Titus. To add to his woes, Paul was about to experience his third shipwreck.

CHAPTER 4

Paul rarely spoke of that third shipwreck, and for good reason. During the ship's two-hundred-mile journey to Troas, torrential rain and strong winds had whipped the ship. Then, just before the ship began entering the Troas harbor, a hard gale struck. The captain ordered all the anchors to be dropped and the sails lowered. For a moment the sea calmed. The ship once more headed for the harbor. Suddenly the winds struck again, this time even harder and more sudden. In the blink of an eye the ship was driven upon the rocky shore and lodged upon the rocks.

If the winds died down again, everyone would be able to safely disembark. The captain urged everyone to stay on board until the passengers could climb down off the ship or be rescued. Paul and three others elected to slip into the water and swim to the nearby shore. It was a decision that saved Paul's life. They plunged into the blue waters of the Aegean Sea and began making their way to shore. An instant later, the ship was hit by a fierce wave. Immediately following, they heard the sound of the ship's timber splintering apart. Exhausted from fighting a merciless sea, Paul pulled himself up on the rocks and waited for the storm to abate. One of the escaping passengers was never accounted for. As to the ship, no evidence of her existence was ever found. A few hours later three half-dead men made their way through the gates leading into Troas.

The next day Paul was informed that the ship, its crew and passengers had, indeed, all perished. As I said, it was a tragedy Paul was reluctant ever to speak of.

(This *third* shipwreck was *not* Paul's last. Another awaited him, three years later, off the coast of Sicily.)

Paul spent his first night in Troas unannounced, in an inn just inside the city. On the morrow, he went straight to the house of one of the Jewish believers. Unceremoniously, Paul's first words were: "Has Titus arrived here?"

"Who is Titus, brother Paul?" came the reply.

Paul's heart sank. "A brother from Antioch," Paul stammered. "He has been with me in Ephesus, but I sent him to the gathering in Corinth. He was to go from Corinth to Philippi and from Philippi to here . . . to Troas. You know of no such person?"

"I have no knowledge of such a person. We will inquire of others, but I doubt your friend is here. We all know when a visiting brother arrives."

That evening a very restless Paul met with the Troas believers. While he was giving them a report of events in Ephesus, a Jewish brother who worked at the harbor came into the room and interrupted Paul. "Troubling news, Paul. I can tell you no more than this: A ship from Corinth has docked here this afternoon. As always, when ships arrive, they bring news. Or, as you know, at least they bring *rumors.* At the time the ship docked, I did not know you were here. I later learned not only of your arrival, but that you were waiting for the arrival of a friend. You can understand, then, what I am about to say, remembering that I thought *you* were in Corinth. What the sailors told me made me think that you, Paul, had been killed in Corinth."

Paul jerked back. "Me? Killed in Corinth? I have not been in Corinth in quite a long time."

"Then it is definitely *only* a rumor," someone said.

"Do you know more?" asked Paul, in near panic.

"Yes, Daggermen from Israel arrived in Corinth and have assassinated *someone* there just a few days ago. It marks the first time Daggermen have struck in Greece."

Paul was confounded. This was news he could not grasp.

The Jewish brother continued: "As we all know, the situation in Israel is grim. Almost every day we hear that the Hebrews may revolt against Rome."

Paul did not hear a word said. For a moment everything went black. A look of horror shot across his face. "Oh, my dear Lord," he began to cry, "could it have been Titus?

"Titus! Titus—is it possible? Have they killed my brother in Christ because they thought it was me?"

"Isn't Titus one of the brothers who has been living with you in Ephesus?" asked one of the sisters. "And was he not once in Jerusalem?" asked someone else.

"Yes, but he is *not* in Antioch or Jerusalem or Ephesus. I sent him to Greece," stammered Paul, still reeling from the news he had just heard. "Titus was to meet me *here*, in Troas, but he is not here. Oh, dear God, please, not Titus! Have I sent that brother to his death?

"I must leave!" Paul announced. "Are there any ships leaving for Philippi tonight?"

Confused, everyone shook their heads at so strange a question.

Nonetheless, that very evening Paul found himself wandering the harbor of Troas, going from one ship to another asking, "Do you sail for Philippi?"

The next few days, while waiting for a ship to depart for Philippi, proved to be among the most dreadful Paul ever lived.

Once he did find a ship bound for Philippi, he called every believer possible to meet him at the port. It was a sad gathering.

The believers in Troas had always expected to greet Paul with great joy should he ever come to visit them. Nonetheless, casting aside their sadness, their prayers for Titus were strong and fervent.

Although Paul promised to return, it was evident his thoughts were centered on Titus.

"If Titus should arrive here, tell him not to move. Somehow, send a message to me in Philippi immediately. In fact, get word to me as soon as you hear *anything.* Wherever Titus is, I pray God that his ship and mine do not pass one another."

Paul added one more word: "Should Titus arrive here, keep him in hiding."

Once on board, Paul, for the first time in his life, asked if there was a private room available. There was, but it was expensive. Nevertheless Paul took it. And there in that room he stayed, fasting and praying, for the entire journey.

Actually Paul did not so much pray as sob. Over and over, almost out of control, he implored his Lord to give protection to Titus. During the long nights that followed his only solace was to walk the ship's deck. Paul was in total despair. He was virtually certain he had been the instrument of Titus's death.

One starless night Paul left his room and looked out over the ship's railing. There, in the deepest moments of his hopelessness, and in a state of utter defeat, the way to end the agony slipped across his mind. That Titus might be dead was more than he could bear. He later described that moment with these words:

"I despaired of life itself."

The voyage to Philippi seemed interminable. When, at last, the ship berthed, Paul was the first person off the ship. As much as his body allowed, he ran all the way from Neapolis to Philippi, going directly to Lydia's home.

As a coincidence, Aquila, Epenetus, and I—along with

Paul's seven friends—had docked only a few hours earlier. We had been in Lydia's home only a few minutes when Paul burst through the door. There was a moment of hesitation. (Paul found it hard to grasp that *Lydia* and *I* could both be in the same room.)

"Oh, you have arrived," was all he said. Then he turned to Lydia: "Titus—has he arrived?" Paul tried to read her eyes, then mine. Not sure what he saw in our eyes, Paul burst into tears.

Lydia immediately rushed to his side and enfolded him in her arms. She was about to say something, but at that very moment Timothy walked into the room. Paul looked up: "Timothy! Is there any word of Titus at all?"

Before Timothy could answer, another voice intruded: "Of course there is. For one thing, I am alive. Furthermore, I did not hear this story about the Daggermen until I arrived here."

Paul whirled around. He blinked in unbelief.

"Brother Paul, though I am a little late in getting here, I bring you good news."

Things were happening too fast. An exhausted Paul simply could not take in either the scene or the words. Almost stumbling, he lunged toward Titus. Titus grabbed him even as both sank to the floor. None of us who were present that day will ever forget it. For several minutes Paul convulsed in Titus's arms. None of us, not even Timothy, had ever seen Paul like this.

Paul ran his trembling hands across Titus's face, then covered that face in kisses, nor did he attempt to speak, for words were beyond his ability. Timothy slid to the floor beside them. He, too, began to cry, but for what reason he did not know.

Finally Paul was able to say, "I heard . . . I heard . . ."

Paul could not finish his sentence. He tried again: "I heard, I heard that you had been killed."

"I know," whispered Titus. "But it was some other uncircumcised heathen, not me." Titus had chosen the exact words to speak, for, despite ourselves, we all began to laugh. Then, beginning to understand the torment Paul had passed through, we gathered around Paul, touched him, held him, and covered him with kisses, all the while weeping profusely.

"I was so sure you were dead," Paul finally said.

"Not me," replied Titus. "Why, in such an indefensible state as that, some Pharisee might have circumcised me!"

Again Paul began to laugh. Once joy arrived, he could not stop the laughter. It was in that moment that healing began.

We hugged again and again; then we all embraced, laughed, then cried, until we were all exhausted. (The ever-beautiful Lydia was an absolute mess, and I was no better.)

Finally Paul managed to stumble his way through a sentence: "Well, young brother not-so-dead-after-all, exactly what is that good news you have? Above all else, is there still an assembly in Corinth? And, by the way, just when did you get here?"

"Yes, oh, brother Paul, yes, yes, yes, there is still an ecclesia in Corinth! And I have been in Philippi about fifteen minutes. It appears we arrived here only moments apart."

For the second time we watched our brother Paul lose complete control. And once more we joined him in our tears.

"I have but one other question, and then, regardless of its answer, we will end this day. I am a man who has not slept in a very long time, nor have I eaten for nearly a week. Quite frankly, I am too old for this kind of business. Titus of Antioch, tell me, am I welcome to return to Corinth, or am I not?"

"You are welcome to return to Corinth! In fact, they are rather angry with you because you have not already returned to them."

Paul, sitting right in the middle of Lydia's living room

floor, began to laugh hysterically. It seemed that those were the last words he could ever have expected. Paul was a man with a good sense of humor, but never had anyone seen him laugh so hard, so long.

"Oh, those Greeks! There's no pleasing them."

We all roared.

Titus said, "I have some very encouraging words for you, Paul. The man who was living with his father's wife has repented and has asked the assembly not only to forgive him but to receive him back. They are awaiting your answer as to what they should do."

"Tell me no more," Paul protested. "Tomorrow, when the sun rises, come to my room and tell me all your news. Now, to sleep."

Paul then gave each of us a warm hug. At last he came to Lydia: "Lydia, you are a sight," he said. "I trust I do not look any worse than you do. Now show me to a room. I die for lack of sleep."

"I shall take you not to *a* room, Paul of Tarsus—I shall take you to *your* room. *That* room is never used by anyone, for any reason. It is yours, it always has been, and it always will be."

So it was that the old warrior, who had recently wrestled with lions in Ephesus, who had been shipwrecked near Troas, and who lived in fear for the life of one of the dearest men in his life, yielded to his humanity. A few moments later, Paul, for the first time in months, fell asleep in the peace of Christ Jesus.

On the morrow, Titus's report to Paul would prove to be fascinating.

CHAPTER 5

There had been no stirring in Paul's room, even after the noon hour. And there was quite a gathering waiting for him: Gaius, Aristarchus, Secundus, Titus, Timothy, Sopater, Tychicus, Trophimus, Epenetus, and Aquila had sat all morning waiting for Paul to come out and speak with them.

"It's the first time ever," observed Timothy.

"And probably the last," replied Tychicus.

"This marks the only time in my life I was up *before* Paul," added Titus.

But the men had not been idle. They had spent most of the morning sharing with one another the events of the last two weeks. Then they had turned to teasing Gaius and Aristarchus, who had become quite the heroes in the eyes of the brothers and sisters in Philippi. And not without justification. Both men had been very bold in their witness for Christ during the Ephesian riot. (Gaius—sure that he would be killed—proclaimed Christ to the mob unceasingly all the way from Tyrannus's house to the amphitheater and even on the theater's stage. The mob, growing disgruntled with his words, began berating him more severely, only to discover that their mistreatment of him provoked him to even greater boldness.)

Those men were a sight to see when they were together, and that morning I noticed that even my dear and ever-quiet Aquila was being corrupted by their wild antics. By noon they were making such a racket that I feared Paul must have died in the night, as their noise would have surely otherwise awakened him.

Having given up on seeing Paul, the men departed for the seaport. A letter had arrived from the province of Galatia stating that five young Galatian men would soon be arriving in Philippi. These five Galatians would be the first of over forty believers to arrive in Philippi on their way to Rome.

(Titus remained, hoping Paul would surely come out of his room shortly.)

All those rowdy men, I thought, *meeting five even younger riotous men from the land of Galatia—what a commotion that will be. Some on their way to Jerusalem, others on their way to Rome. What a clatter that will make in Lydia's household!*

Lydia and I spent the next few hours sharing our life stories with one another. Paul had once said to me: "Priscilla, you will find in Lydia a woman not unlike yourself. The two of you have much in common, both in experience *and* in disposition." His words were true. A bond between us was born that day, which has never been severed.

Some hours later we heard a noise coming from Paul's room. A moment later he emerged, his face swollen, his steps unsure. I hardly recognized him except for his beaming smile.

Paul asked, "Where is Titus? What hour is it?"

"Titus is in his room awaiting your call. As to what hour it is—all Philippians will be going to bed very soon," laughed Lydia.

Paul was shocked. He gasped and said, "I've *never* slept this long!"

"That is reasonable," she responded. "You have never been

this exhausted. A shipwreck, a week without food, things like that do tend to affect us mortals."

A few moments later Paul was consuming a hearty meal of fruit, bread, and goat cheese.

"And now . . . Titus. He said things were well in Corinth did he not? Or was that one of my dreams?"

"Those were his words," replied Lydia.

"Then I will spend what remains of this day listening to his report."

With that, one of Lydia's servants made off in the direction of Titus's room. The two men spent the next hours discussing not only Corinth but also Thessalonica and Berea, for Titus had managed to briefly visit both those cities on his way up to Philippi.

"There were four factions in Corinth when you wrote to them. I am pleased to inform you that today there are only *two!* There are those who want you to return and those who do *not* want you to return!"

Paul smiled knowingly and took Titus's words as genuine good news. Titus's brow furrowed as he continued: "They know about Blastinius. He was there. So were his cohorts."

"I had assumed as much," replied Paul. "What did he say? What did he do? Just what does that man do when he goes after me, after my reputation, after the churches?"

"That is a very interesting question, Paul. Blastinius never met with the Corinthian assembly. Nor *any* believers. Blastinius knew he would get nowhere with his stories about you. Even Corinth has outgrown that kind of criticism about you. Rather, Blastinius spent his time with the synagogue leaders. He has utterly turned away from the gospel and is championing the Law. Blastinius has a new strategy. He goes to the legalistic Jews, while his traveling companions go to the believers. When meeting with one of the assemblies, his friends do

25

exactly what they did in Antioch. They come to the meetings, befriend people, and then, gradually, they begin to undermine you, your reputation, and your message."

"And?" queried Paul.

Titus broke out in a very satisfied grin. "It didn't work! Well, that is, they did not do the kind of damage they hoped for. But they did manage to plant seeds of doubt about you. On the other hand, most everyone remembered that Peter came to Corinth at your request. That fact counterbalanced the criticism launched against you by the Jerusalem visitors."

Paul nodded.

"Oh, Paul, do you remember when Blastinius first went to Galatia, and he had a letter of approval from Jerusalem?"

Paul grunted sullenly.

"Well, you will find this hard to believe, but those men are *still* brandishing around that letter from James."

"No!" replied a stunned Paul. "I did not think that even a man like Blastinius would sink *that* low . . . not after the apostles and elders in Jerusalem sent so clear a letter of endorsement to the Antioch church. What else?"

"As I told you yesterday, the brother living in incest has repented and asked to be allowed back into the assembly. *This* time the church is awaiting your decision on this matter."

"As it should. What more?" asked Paul.

"The Jerusalem visitors continue to condemn you for not receiving money for your ministry. And that fact—that you do not take money—*still* does not sit well with *some* in Corinth."

"I will never understand!" declared a bewildered Paul. "Never! I *cannot* believe it. Criticized for *not* taking money." For a short time Paul sat staring blankly at the floor.

"And the Daggermen? Are they still in Corinth?"

"*This* is not good news. Yes, they came to Corinth. And

even *now* they are trying to locate you. And yes, they wish to . . . end your life."

Paul said, "Blastinius has done his job well. He has been true to his vow, has he not? There is no reason for the *sicarii* [which being translated means Daggermen] to count me as an enemy of Israel, and certainly no reason to come all the way to southern Greece to kill me. Am I the only one they seek *outside* of Israel?"

"We have heard that one or two Daggermen have been sent to Rome. In *that* case, it is a suicide pact on the part of those who are bound for Rome. When they came to Corinth and could not find you, they did not waste their trip. They found the most influential Roman businessman in Corinth and assassinated him!"

Paul blinked, bowed his head, but said nothing.

Titus said, "Another word about Blastinius—this you need to know. Whatever city he enters, he asks the local Jews to tell him of any other towns that have a synagogue. He also collects the names of the Jewish leaders in those towns. He then writes letters to the synagogues and these men, warning them about you!"

"Unbelievable," groaned Paul. "I have referred to Blastinius as a thorn in my flesh. Should I not call it a *dagger?!*"

Paul sighed: "It seems obvious that I must now write another letter to Corinth. We should begin immediately."

It was summer. Twenty-seven years had passed since the Resurrection and Pentecost.

True to his word, Paul began making notes for the letter to Corinth that evening by torchlight.

CHAPTER 6

Titus, the last time I was in Jerusalem, Peter informed me that a drought had been going on there for several years," said Paul. "Peter felt that if the drought continued much longer, the poorest of the Jewish believers would suffer greatly. There is yet another reason that causes this to be even a greater crisis than it ought to be. The men who control the Temple treasury refuse to allow any money to be used to help poor people who are believers. The poor who do not acknowledge Christ receive help. The poor who live in the villages and towns in Israel are moving to Jerusalem, but when followers of the Lord arrive, they receive no help.

"I knew, as soon as Peter told me this, the Gentile churches *must* come to the aid of the Jewish poor. We will soon be on our way to Jerusalem and as we do we will choose a route that takes us through the Gentile provinces. We will be receiving money from the Gentile churches for these needy Hebrew brothers and sisters.

"We will pass through Greece, Asia Minor, Galatia, and Syria on our way to Jerusalem. Each of you brothers will personally take the money that was given in *your* home province."

"Who will collect the money from Corinth?" asked Titus. "We eight come from everywhere *except* southern Greece."

"*I* will carry the Corinthian gift," answered Paul, knowing full well his answer would be a surprising one. Aquila and I, as well as everyone else who worked with Paul, knew that he *never* touched money.

"In southern Greece only the towns of Cenchrea and Corinth have assemblies. And, yes, you are correct, there are no workers among us from southern Greece. It falls to me to receive their gift. Furthermore, I want Corinth to know that *I* trust Corinth to trust *me!*"

"When do we leave?" asked Gaius, walking into the room.

Paul looked up. "Not until the forty brothers and sisters have all arrived here safely. Once they all arrive, I desire to see them off personally to Rome."

"The church that will soon begin in Rome will be a strong church from day one!" added Timothy, stepping into the room.

"Where have you men been all day?" asked Paul, as he watched the entire troupe file into his room.

"At the docks. We are expecting the first arrivals from Galatia."

"How will we reach Jerusalem?" asked Trophimus. "By land or sea?"

"Overland as much as possible, except, of course, from Philippi to Asia Minor.

"You are an inquisitive lot, tonight. You do realize you have interrupted an important meeting. I am about to attempt to write another letter to Corinth. A young man is on his way here right now to assist me. An *amanuensis* [or scribe]. He is someone Lydia has recommended. His name is Tertius."

"Good!" exclaimed Timothy. "I hope you always use him! I have been considering the possibility of breaking my hand."

As usual, Paul ignored the levity and moved on. "When Tertius arrives, he and I will make some notes; then, if he is as good as Lydia says, I will begin the letter."

For the next hour the eight men pelted Paul with questions. Paul, who had wished to be alone with Titus, finally relaxed into the conversation.

Shortly thereafter, Lydia's servants brought a sumptuous meal into the dining room. It was quite a remarkable gathering that sat down to dine together. After offering thanks to God for his safekeeping of Titus, we lifted our entreaties to God to keep safe all of those who were on their way to Philippi. We then prayed for the people of Rome, ending with a prayer concerning our future on Aventine Hill, the location of the home I had bought there.

A few moments into the meal, Tertius arrived. Originally this young man had come from southern Greece but had moved to Philippi to ply his trade as a scribe. Tertius was a master of both Greek and Latin and could write faster than I ever dreamed humanly possible. Further, in the examples he presented us, his script was straight, clear, and beautiful. So also, his speech. My first thought was, How could a man so young be so brilliant? Tertius had been meeting with the gathering in Philippi for several years. It was Lydia who had introduced him to an indwelling Lord. We all took to him immediately.

"If you will excuse me," said Paul, as he stood.

A few moments later the brothers, including Titus, also excused themselves. Paul returned to his room; Tertius and Timothy followed him. The other brothers made another trip out to the port to see if a ship might have come in bearing five scruffy young men from Galatia.

"I believe this brother will prove to be adequate—perhaps even better than you, Timothy."

"I am heartbroken," replied Timothy, beaming as he spoke, for he hated being Paul's letter writer. He then turned to Tertius. "May I watch how you do this?"

"Of course," replied Tertius.

First Tertius selected two sheets of papyrus. He then carefully smoothed them out with a piece of ivory.

"I thought *pumice stone* was better than ivory for doing that," Timothy commented. "I understand ivory can sometimes make the paper too shiny for the ink, unless it is done very carefully."

"You are correct," said Tertius, smiling. "But I *am* careful." When Tertius had finished smoothing the pages, he folded each of the two sheets from top to bottom. "Now I have *four* pages," he said as he finished. Timothy noted the sheets had been ten inches wide, and—now that they were folded—each page was five inches wide. Tertius reached into his pouch and drew out a small piece of lead, which he used to draw a fine, barely visible, margin around the edge of each of the four pages.

"Timothy, could you move back just a little?"

Timothy quickly leaned back. Tertius then drew twenty-four horizontal lines on each page. These lines were so faint Timothy could hardly see them. Twenty-four lines on each page, with a margin *around* each page. Tertius returned to his pouch and drew out a reed. He cut the reed at one end. Not happy with the result, he picked out a stone and with the stone sharpened the end of the reed.

"This reed comes from a lake in Asia, famed for producing high-quality reeds."

"Tertius, . . . what is that ink made from?" asked a still curious Timothy.

Tertius lifted his ceramic pot, placing it carefully on the table before him and removing the seal. "This ink is a combination of soot, carbon from a fireplace, and gummy water. If I make a mistake and if the ink is still wet, I can wipe the ink off with this damp sponge. But, as you know, once the ink has dried it is there forever." To illustrate, Tertius drew some practice strokes. Then, using his sponge, he wiped them away.

"Oh, is that how it's done? . . ." mused Timothy.

"Why," Tertius looked up, "what do you use?"

Timothy began to stammer out some vague response, but, to his relief, Paul broke in: "Tertius, how fast—or slow—should I speak?"

Tertius responded with a quotation only a few amanuenses could make: "*celeritatem linguae manus sequitur . . .*"

Paul smiled; Timothy was lost.

Tertius continued and said, "It is a saying only a few amanuenses can truthfully make. It means I am capable of using symbols instead of words. Consequently, I can write much faster than an amanuensis who must write out every word. I can match the speed of any speaker. That is, I can write as fast as Paul can speak. What I do is called *semiographos*. The word means 'symbol writing.' Few can do this. When Paul is finished speaking, I will rewrite those symbols into words. Timothy, how fast can you write?"

Timothy blushed and, with his face begging for help, looked at Paul.

Paul laid his hand on Timothy's shoulder and said, "Not *quite* as fast as you." Paul paused. "Timothy's native language is the dialect of Lyconia. Greek is his second language."

I have to confess that I wanted very much to be present with the three men, to hear what Paul would say in his letter to Corinth. (Later, Paul was gracious enough to invite both Lydia and me to hear a large part of the letter.)

And so they began.

Perhaps, dear reader, you are familiar with this letter?

Copies of Paul's letter to Corinth have since been made and passed out among several of the churches in Greece. A few copies have even reached as far south as Asia Minor and Galatia. What follows now, is the story behind Paul's letter.

CHAPTER 7

Tertius, this is how I wish to open the letter."

"Say on," replied Tertius, as he dipped his reed into the ink.

This letter is from Paul, appointed by God to be an apostle of Christ Jesus, and from our dear brother Timothy.

We are writing to God's church in Corinth and to all the Christians throughout Greece.

May God our Father and the Lord Jesus Christ give you his grace and peace.

All praise to the God and Father of our Lord Jesus Christ. He is the source of every mercy and the God who comforts us. He comforts us in all our troubles so that we can comfort others. When others are troubled, we will be able to give them the same comfort God has given us. You can be sure that the more we suffer for Christ, the more God will shower us with his comfort through Christ. So when we are weighed down with troubles, it is for your benefit and salvation! For when God comforts us, it is so that we, in turn, can be an encouragement to you. Then you can patiently endure the same things we suffer. We are confident that as you share in suffering, you will also share God's comfort.

Timothy began to realize Paul was writing a letter far more personal than any of his previous letters. Just how personal became evident about eleven pages later.

"I must tell them," breathed Paul, ". . . I must tell them a little of the dark waters I have passed through of late."

"A great deal has happened in the three months since you wrote the earlier letter. Why not tell them about those three months?" urged Timothy. "They should know. The riot in Ephesus . . . the disappearance of Titus . . . Blastinius . . . the Daggermen!"

Paul pondered the idea. "Perhaps. Yes, I suppose when you get very old, you have the right to make a few personal references." For the very first time, Paul opened his heart—a little—and began to relate some of the excruciating pain he had recently endured.

> I think you ought to know, dear brothers and sisters, about the trouble we went through in the province of Asia. We were crushed and completely overwhelmed, and we thought we would never live through it.

Paul went on to declare to the Corinthians that through all the hardships God was faithful and sustained him. He also thanked them for their prayers for his safety.

While Paul searched his mind as to what to say next, Tertius spoke. "In my notes you asked me to remind you to tell the Corinthians why you had not been able to come to them at the time you had promised."

"Yes," replied Paul. "And please, Tertius, if you will, continue to keep a watchful eye on our notes."

> We can say with confidence and a clear conscience that we have been honest and sincere in all our dealings. We have depended on God's grace, not on our own earthly wisdom. That is how we have acted toward everyone, and especially

toward you. My letters have been straightforward, and there is nothing written between the lines and nothing you can't understand. I hope someday you will fully understand us, even if you don't fully understand us now. Then on the day when our Lord Jesus comes back again, you will be proud of us in the same way we are proud of you.

Since I was so sure of your understanding and trust, I wanted to give you a double blessing. I wanted to stop and see you on my way to Macedonia and again on my return trip. Then you could send me on my way to Judea.

You may be asking why I changed my plan. Hadn't I made up my mind yet? Or am I like people of the world who say yes when they really mean no? As surely as God is true, I am not that sort of person. My yes means yes because Jesus Christ, the Son of God, never wavers between yes and no. He is the one whom Timothy, Silas, and I preached to you, and he is the divine Yes—God's affirmation. For all of God's promises have been fulfilled in him. That is why we say "Amen" when we give glory to God through Christ. It is God who gives us, along with you, the ability to stand firm for Christ. He has commissioned us, and he has identified us as his own by placing the Holy Spirit in our hearts as the first installment of everything he will give us.

Now I call upon God as my witness that I am telling the truth. The reason I didn't return to Corinth was to spare you from a severe rebuke. But that does not mean we want to tell you exactly how to put your faith into practice. We want to work together with you so you will be full of joy as you stand firm in your faith.

I am quite sure that the Corinthians were taken aback to discover Paul's reason for not having returned to Corinth sooner. That surprise must have grown even greater as they read what Paul wrote next.

That is why I wrote as I did in my last letter, so that when I do come, I will not be made sad by the very ones who ought to give me the greatest joy. Surely you know that my happiness depends on your happiness.

"Tertius, I owe you an explanation," said Paul, as he leaned back to rest for a moment. "There has been a great deal of pain experienced both on my part and on the part of the Corinthians. A man in the assembly there was living with his father's wife! Incest! The church was doing nothing about it. I despise what I am about to write. I have no desire to shame the Corinthians any more than they have already been shamed."

Paul breathed hard as he signaled Tertius to write again.

How painful it was to write that letter! Heartbroken, I cried over it. I didn't want to hurt you, but I wanted you to know how very much I love you.

I am not overstating it when I say that the man who caused all the trouble hurt your entire church more than he hurt me. He was punished enough when most of you were united in your judgment against him. Now it is time to forgive him and comfort him. Otherwise he may become so discouraged that he won't be able to recover. Now show him that you still love him.

I wrote to you as I did to find out how far you would go in obeying me. When you forgive this man, I forgive him, too. And when I forgive him (for whatever is to be forgiven), I do so with Christ's authority for your benefit, so that Satan will not outsmart us. For we are very familiar with his evil schemes.

At that point Paul released a deep sigh, as a man who had just laid down a heavy load.

"It is late. That is enough for tonight. We are all tired."

Nonetheless, Paul continued speaking, but it was more to himself than to Timothy or Tertius.

"Shall I tell the Corinthians *all* I have been through since I wrote that letter? The rumors—the ones I have heard—the one *they* have heard?! That I feared for Titus's life when I arrived in Troas and he was not there? Dare I speak of Blastinius Drachrachma . . . after all these years? I have *never* spoken of him before! Surely the Lord will make these things clear to me on the morrow."

Paul looked up and said, "Timothy, tomorrow—if I decide to do this—then I believe that I shall also do something else that I have never done previously. It might be good to have the other brothers and sisters sit with us. Tertius, I trust you are not bothered by a room full of people."

"Not at all."

"Then tomorrow we shall continue this letter. Tertius, meet with me at the first light of the sun. Timothy, tell Titus that tomorrow I shall not oversleep."

Paul was true to his word. The next morning he was up very early. Further, he *did* decide to invite an entire roomful of us to listen as he spoke and Tertius wrote. And what a letter it was . . . despite the fact that we were interrupted. *Very* interrupted.

CHAPTER 8

Just as we were gathering to join Paul, there was a noisy knock at the door. When Lydia opened the door, there stood five very excited young men. They unceremoniously burst in, hugged Lydia, and began talking all as one. They were exuberant about everything, but especially about all they had seen while walking from the port to Philippi. They wanted to tell us about everything that had happened to them since leaving Galatia.

"Two months ago I was a slave," announced one, loudly. "Now look at me! I am traveling the empire." The young man's name was Asyncritus.

"Three months ago we were *all* slaves," chimed a brother named Patrobas.

And so the excited chatter went . . . for hours . . . and days . . . and weeks! The Galatian brothers had arrived, the first of the Gentile ecclesia travelers planning to journey to Rome and help with the planting of the new assembly there. I pulled Lydia aside for a whispered conversation. Lydia signalled for her servant. Then, interrupting the loud ruckus, Lydia said, "Surely you must be hungry from your travels; we've just finished eating our morning meal, but I will have my servants bring some food for you."

Paul had stepped out of his room to discover the reason for

the commotion. As he did, all five young men grabbed him and began passing him from one brother to another, all the while shouting greetings to him from their home churches.

Eventually we were able to settle them down enough to hear their report on the Galatian churches. Servants arrived with a sumptuous meal for the newly arrived travelers. The young men's eyes glistened in anticipation of the feast. I smiled and nodded at Lydia. One of the enthusiastic storytellers blessed the food, and the tales continued as they began eating.

These men *had walked* virtually the entire journey from Galatia to Greece. Everything they had seen had held them spellbound. The reason for their exuberance was simple enough to understand: Until a few weeks ago *all five* had been *slaves*. Most of them had never been over five miles from home. Their masters, also believers, had set them free for the purpose of letting them go to Rome to be part of the birth of the assembly there.

(I must tell you that I fell in love with every one of them.)

For an hour or so, they regaled us with stories of how they often got lost. Soldiers had almost arrested them once. They became sick from eating strange food. They marveled as they told of the hospitality they received from believers as they traveled northward from one city to another. All this they told with such energy that we could not help but laugh, cry, and love. Even Lydia lost her reserved demeanor as these young men entertained us with one tale after another.

After my many years in the life of the ecclesia, I tell you that there really is nothing on this earth quite like young believers in Christ, especially believers of this stripe.

Paul plied them with questions about each of the four churches in Galatia *and* about the new assemblies that were being born there. We could see the enormous satisfaction Paul had as he learned that the number of believers and the number of churches were increasing.

At that point Paul surprised and delighted the young men.

"Priscilla and Aquila will leave in a few days for Rome. I want them to have enough time in Rome to prepare to receive a large number of guests. Even now about forty believers are on their way to Rome by way of Philippi. But I would like for you five to *not* wait until the others arrive. I want you to go to Rome with Priscilla, Aquila, and Epenetus. They will need you to help them."

Once again the young men erupted into wild delight.

"How do you get to Rome from here?" asked Phlegon.

"We will travel west, overland, until we reach the Adriatic Sea. We will arrive at a seaport city called Dyrrhachium," explained Paul.

"Dyrrhachium is Greece's port city for reaching Italy. From Dyrrhachium we will sail across the Adriatic to the Italian city of Brundisium," continued Aquila.

I added, "From Brundisium, we will either walk four hundred miles northward . . . or we will take a ship."

"Priscilla has purchased a home in Rome. *That* is your destination," Paul informed them.

Once more the young men were awed.

Later, they deluged me with questions about Rome, my home on Aventine Hill, the emperor . . . *everything*. When I explained the size of Rome, the streets, the noise, the location of the house, I saw that they had no way to comprehend what I was describing.

"I will be asking you brothers *not* to make your home on Aventine Hill," instructed Paul. "First of all, you cannot afford to live there, as you will be earning not much more than slave wages."

"Slave wages? There is no such thing as slaves having wages!" said Asyncritus. The other four roared with laughter.

"We know all this," said an ebullient Hermas. "What is your second request?"

"I would like for you five to move into an *insula*. That is, a rented room in a huge building called an *island*. Once there you must form a *koinonia*."

The young men stared at Paul. "What is an insula?" one asked. I asked if I might explain.

"Please do," responded Paul.

"Almost all of the city of Rome is made up of long brick buildings, which are usually five stories high. These 'insulae' are dark and horrible, and they stink. They are but a series of rooms that have no windows and little ventilation. They are too hot in the summer and too cold in the winter. People who rent them always try to get a room on the top floor—or if they cannot, the bottom floor.

"All five of you brothers together will probably be able to afford to rent just one small room. The room will be no more than eight feet by eight feet. If you do as most Romans, you will use the room mostly as a place to keep your belongings and your food. An insula is too miserable to sleep in. Most people sleep on the roof or outdoors in a forum. People sleep inside only when it is very cold or when there is a storm," I said and paused. The five men had no negative reactions.

"Italians are a minority in Rome, but they have an attitude you will immediately recognize. Every Italian man thinks he is the most handsome man in the world and that he can sing better than anyone else on earth . . . *and* quote poetry more magnificently than anyone else. Further, every one of them considers himself the greatest philosopher of all time."

Paul began to laugh. "I thought only a Greek held such a high view of himself!"

"Singing, poetry, and arguments help make Rome the noisiest place in the world . . . during the day." I continued,

"Because of the terrible living conditions in the insulae, virtually everyone lives *outside* all day. The conditions in Rome are crowded beyond anything you can imagine. Worse, during the days, along the sides of every street *everyone* is there trying to sell you something. Men sit out in the open eighteen hours a day hoping to make *one* sale. The goal of every man is to make *one* denarius a day. It is a good day indeed when a man can make as much as *two* denarii. The final mix of all these elements is . . . *total* chaos. At night, not only are the forums packed with sleeping people, so are the side streets.

"Every morning during winter, you will be seeing bodies hauled out of the city in wagons. The life span of the poor in Rome is very short. And almost everyone in Rome *is* poor—*very* poor. Disease is rampant. Plagues are frequent."

"What about famine? How often is there a famine?" asked one of the young men, so used to that scourge in his own land.

"This is the only good word I can say of Rome. There might be famine all over the world, but *never* in Rome. Most of the ships that dock in the seaports near Rome are bringing grain . . . specifically for Rome. There are no bread riots in Rome. There is *always* grain, even when the rest of the provinces are starving."

Still, none of this impressed the Galatian brothers. They were, after all, from perhaps the poorest area of the empire.

"What is *koinonia*, brother Paul?" asked one of the brothers, "You asked us to form a koinonia. Am I supposed to know what a koinonia is?"

"Better you ask Priscilla," replied Paul. "She can give you a more informed answer."

"There are several ways to survive in Rome. These have evolved over the centuries," I replied. "The tradesmen have joined together in *guilds*. Others join together for mutual survival because of their commonly held *political* views. Others band together to help one another survive based on some shared philosophy of life. All have one thing in common: They are workers who pool their money and other resources in order to rent a small room in one of the insulae! They all work long *and* hard just to pay the rent and buy food. They live, they work, they share their food, their room, their *everything* . . . just to stay alive. And they continue to do this all the rest of their lives.

"Then there is one other group. This group is called a 'koinonia.' These are people who have no common interest whatsoever. They may be of many different trades, backgrounds, tribes, races, languages, or cultures. Survival is their only purpose in joining together."

"Sounds something like the Lord's assemblies," observed Titus. "We are of every assortment imaginable, and because of Christ we hold onto one another."

"It is a good word," mused Paul. "We *koinonia* together for the sake and glory of Jesus Christ."

"Is there more for us to know, sister Priscilla?" asked Phlegon.

"Yes, you need to know that there are fourteen districts in Rome. The Trastavere district is the poorest of all. It is the *only* district you can afford to live in."

One of the young Galatians shot his fist into the air: "Trastavere is for us!"

"It is also the area of the city where, by law, the Jews *must* live. That is, until Claudius ordered all Jews to leave Rome. Sometimes wealthy Jews succeeded in moving out of that district. If one is wealthy enough, the law is ignored. Otherwise, if you are Jewish, you live in the Trastavere ghetto."

Everyone looked over at my husband, Aquila.

"He married *me*," I said proudly. "Therefore Aquila can live in the Aventine district."

"She *thinks* I married her for love," replied Aquila dryly.

Not to be outdone, I responded: "And I married Aquila for his beautiful head of hair," running my fingers across his thinning hairline as I spoke.

Returning to the subject, I added: "What the Trastavere district looks like today, I cannot say. There are no Jews there—not since Claudius and his decree. I assume the *very* poor have moved there and taken over the entire district. Its one and only bright spot is that it is near the Aventine district. The Aventine district is just north of Trastavere. They are separated only by the Tiber River; a bridge joins them."

"You do realize you will be paid very little for your labor, do you not?" asked Paul. "Together, you may be able to afford a room. Try to find a *large* room . . . with a window, if such a room exists."

"Can we afford a *large* room?" asked Asyncritus.

"Probably not," responded Paul, "not for long. But remember, during the next few months there are going to be other young men coming into Rome in order to be part of the Lord's assembly. When these brothers arrive, they will need a place to stay until they find work. You are their pathfinders. Because you will have work and will understand the maze of Roman streets, you will be able to help these arrivals to also find work."

The five young men beamed!

"According to what Priscilla has told me, there is one thing that is unique to Rome. It is the only city on earth where you may be able to find employment that lasts all year long."

The mouths of the five young men dropped open.

"You mean you can work *every day*—you do not have to go to the marketplace and wait to be hired . . . day by day?"

"I realize it sounds strange. I, too, have a hard time imagining such a thing," replied Paul.

"Working *every* day," said Hermas slowly.

"It is not as wonderful as you might think," I replied wryly.

"May I remind you that the working conditions in Rome are quite terrible. And every day means *every* day of the year. The only time you may have a free day will be during the heathen festivals. Nonetheless, I will do all that is in my power to help you find work that is not as destructive to your bodies as is most employment."

"I can plough!" said Patrobas.

"There are no farms inside the city of Rome," said Aquila, amused at the young man's words.

"Oh," Patrobas replied. "I forgot."

I sighed deeply, sad in knowing my next words would *not* be understood.

"The worst problem that faces *all* who live in Rome is *getting a night's sleep!* There is racket, screaming, and arguing all night. Add to that the wails of those begging for alms. The din *never* ends. In the day it is the unrelenting noise of people; then, when night comes, the city gates are opened, and thousands upon thousands of cattle, sheep, goats, ducks, and every other imaginable creature is driven *into* the city. With all that noise there is added yet more yelling and screaming. Roman nights are the hardest of all to endure."

"From all that Priscilla has told me, I would never go there . . . except that it is the capital of the world," inserted Paul. "Therefore, I *must* go."

"We will assuredly survive," responded Hermes. "We will go to the Trastavere district. We will find a *large* room. We will work hard, and we will await the coming of other young men like us."

"And," added Asyncritus, "we will be the first young single brothers to be part of the church that gathers in Rome!"

"Not only that, we shall have a great koinonia in Christ," exuded Patrobas.

"Fear, Nero, fear! Young single brothers are marching on

Rome!" declared Tychicus, who was, at the same time, laughing almost hysterically.

"I remind you, please do not stay long in Priscilla's home," urged Paul. "About thirty-five to forty more brothers and sisters will arrive there a few weeks after you do."

I, Priscilla, was a little concerned about Paul's wanting to make sure those five young men did not become a burden to me in my home—and I said so. Paul was about to reply but remembered that Lydia was in the room. Knowing his certain defeat, Paul chose, wisely, to say no more.

"You will have to forgive us," said Paul, "but I have much to do yet this morning. I have set aside the day for the writing of a letter to Corinth."

With a round of strong embraces and wild declarations the five rowdy young men departed. One of Lydia's servants had promised to show them the jail where Paul and Silas had been beaten, imprisoned, and then liberated by an earthquake. They were in awe at the thought of seeing such a place, for the story of that night had become legend among the Gentile churches.

"You will all be interested to know," said Lydia, "that jail is no longer used for imprisonment. After the earthquake it was deemed unusable as a prison."

Paul, having no previous knowledge of that fact, raised both hands in praise. "I *must* send word to Silas. He will be delighted to hear such news. So also will his *back*.

"Come, Aquila, come Priscilla, let's get back to that letter. You have lived in Corinth. You have also come to know that, for a long time, I have a very committed enemy who follows me wherever I go, seeking to destroy any and all of the churches that have been raised up by my hand."

"Yes," I replied, "but you also know that we have never asked anything about this man. We have known that it was your desire never to speak of him. Until today we have never known his name."

"Good!" exclaimed Paul. "But now the Corinthians know him! He has, at last, come even to Corinth and done all in his power to ravage the assembly in Corinth as well as the one in Cenchrea."

So it was that Lydia, Timothy, Titus, Aquila, and I, along with the amanuensis Tertius, once more sat down in Paul's room to hear him dictate the remainder of that most incredible letter.

CHAPTER 9

"On three occasions I have gone to the Lord with pleadings, asking him to remove Blastinius Drachrachma from my life," said Paul.

"Years ago I wrote the Galatian letter," he added pensively. "The man who sits here with you today is not the man who dictated *that* letter. I have changed. That is, *Blastinius* has changed me. As much as I am loathe to admit it, Blastinius *is* God's will for my life. He and his many cohorts have done me great damage—or so it seems from an earthly viewpoint. You all know the charges he and others bring against me: that I have not been sent of God to raise up assemblies in the land of the Gentiles; that I am a renegade apostle, a destroyer of the Mosaic covenant; and," Paul winced, "that I am not well-educated.

"Then there is that *other* charge. It is one that is beyond me to comprehend. This business of my not taking money has galled almost everyone. My entire ministry as a *sent one* . . . sent by God to the Gentiles . . . my testimony . . . has been made of no account just because I do not take money." Paul laughed at the irony.

"Men were bound to find something in my life to criticize. But *not taking money?* I still do not understand."

For a moment Paul stared blankly into space, then quickly

added, "The Lord has delivered me from the pain that I felt at the time Blastinius first entered my life. Today I am at peace. *God* sent that man to me."

Paul grimaced "But . . . *not* taking money!" He threw up his hands in dismay. He fell silent once more, then declared, "What does still gall me is that these men speak of me as someone *not* well-educated!"

Every person in that room knew there was probably not a man living in the entire world who was more familiar with history, philosophy, culture, and many other facts of life. Nor was there a Pharisee, Sadducee, or scribe breathing who could best Paul in his understanding of the ancient Hebrew scriptures. We immediately understood Paul's pain. To be referred to as not well-educated must have hurt deeply.

I must add that our brother Paul was not only very knowledgeable, he had something more than a great mind. He had a revelation of an indwelling Christ. It was a revelation of Christ that—dare I say—may have gone beyond even that of the Twelve. The Twelve were very familiar with the Christ who walked the streets of Israel those three years. But Paul was very familiar with the ascended Christ who reigned enthroned—and who dwells within us.

At that point Paul turned once more to Tertius. Oblivious to everyone in the room, he continued touching on incredible stories from his life.

Speaking first of the most recent events, Paul began that part of the letter by alluding to Titus's disappearance.

> Well, when I came to the city of Troas to preach the Good News of Christ, the Lord gave me tremendous opportunities.
>
> But I couldn't rest because my dear brother Titus hadn't yet arrived with a report from you. So I said good-bye and went on to Macedonia to find him.

Paul continued for a moment, thanking God for Titus and for the Corinthian church. Then with eyes sparkling, "Ah, now it is *I*, not Blastinius, who will talk about *letters*. Blastinius made a great point of the importance of having a letter—a letter of commendation! I will now speak on this subject."

With that Paul turned the tables on Blastinius, a man so skillful in charging that Paul had no letter of commendation. Oh, what Paul had to say about *that!*

Are we beginning again to tell you how good we are? Some people need to bring letters of recommendation with them or ask you to write letters of recommendation for them. But the only letter of recommendation we need is you yourselves! Your lives are a letter written in our hearts, and everyone can read it and recognize our good work among you. Clearly, you are a letter from Christ prepared by us. It is written not with pen and ink, but with the Spirit of the living God. It is carved not on stone, but on human hearts.

We are confident of all this because of our great trust in God through Christ. It is not that we think we can do anything of lasting value by ourselves. Our only power and success come from God. He is the one who has enabled us to represent his new covenant. This is a covenant, not of written laws, but of the Spirit. The old way ends in death; in the new way, the Holy Spirit gives life.

As Paul finished those last words, I was breathless. So also were the others in the room. Paul had taken the concept of the letter of the law and, to the exaltation of Jesus Christ, compared that letter with the letter of the Spirit . . . and the living letters . . . the assemblies!

He then took up another issue raised by Blastinius, that is, the superiority of the covenant that God gave Moses. Paul had Tertius write of how those who read the words of Moses have a veil over their hearts and eyes. Yet when they turn to Christ, that veil is lifted.

Paul continued using the word *we*, but, as I listened, I only heard *I*. Paul's *we* was a reference to himself: We do not try to trick anyone, and we do not distort the Word of God.

After that Paul spoke of veiled eyes, eyes that do not see the glory of the Christ who is the exact likeness of God. Then he made another oblique reference to Blastinius, for Blastinius had often boasted about himself, about the law, about *his* letter of commendation, about his education. This boasting on the part of Blastinius had caused a number of believers to doubt Paul's validity as a worker.

> We don't go around preaching about ourselves; we preach Christ Jesus, the Lord.

For the next two or three minutes, Paul's words had devastation in them, yet, he brought the church in Corinth back to the Lord Jesus.

From that point on, Paul used the plural *we* exclusively. Why did he do this? Paul was including the sufferings of Silas and the faithfulness of Timothy. Or was it that he could not bring himself to say *I*. For whatever reason, the truth is *we* really was an *I*.

Little by little Paul continued to venture out into details of his experiences.

> We are pressed on every side by troubles, but we are not crushed and broken. We are perplexed, but we don't give up and quit. We are hunted down, but God never abandons us. We get knocked down, but we get up again and keep going. Through suffering, these bodies of ours constantly share in the death of Jesus so that the life of Jesus may also be seen in our bodies.
>
> Yes, we live under constant danger of death because we

serve Jesus, so that the life of Jesus will be obvious in our dying bodies. So we live in the face of death, but it has resulted in eternal life for you.

What Paul was doing, it became evident, was showing the Corinthians his attitude toward criticism, his attitude toward the many troubles he faced, and, at the same time, without saying it, reminding the Corinthians of *their* thin skin. Their quickness to squabble, to be offended, was something even they were very conscious of.

For our present troubles are quite small and won't last very long. Yet they produce for us an immeasurably great glory that will last forever!

As Paul spoke, and as Tertius wrote, more intimate details of Paul's life were being revealed.

I cannot tell you how moved I became in hearing the words that followed. Here was a confession from Paul concerning the constant possibility of dying, yet even *this* he turned to the glory of the Lord Jesus. Above all else, one thing came across clearly: This man was in no way afraid of death.

Yes, we are fully confident, and we would rather be away from these bodies, for then we will be at home with the Lord.

Paul paused a moment. You could see a little restlessness in him as he paused.

"Am I bragging?" he asked the Corinthians rhetorically. "No, I am just talking to you so that you might have some pride concerning this one who has worked among you."

In the words that followed Paul again said *we*, but I heard the *we* as meaning Paul.

If it seems that we are crazy, it is to bring glory to God.

He then quickly added,

And if we are in our right minds, it is for your benefit. What-ever we do, it is because Christ's love controls us. Since we be-lieve that Christ died for everyone, we also believe that we have all died to the old life we used to live.

"And if we are in our right minds, it is for your benefit. Whatever I do, I do it because I am constrained by Christ," Paul said under his breath.

As before, Paul's thoughts moved on to the glory of his Lord, ending with these words:

For God made Christ, who never sinned, to be the offering for our sin, so that we could be made right with God through Christ.

There was a pause, and silence hung in the air. I, Priscilla, dared to break the silence.

"Brother Paul, somewhere in this letter you should be even more specific about the deep waters you have passed through. Until now, you have spoken in general terms concerning your suffering in Christ. Please, be specific."

I was suddenly interrupted by Timothy. He said, "I agree. If Silas were here, he would agree as well. You have *never* fully told what you have gone through in bringing the gospel to Galatia or to northern Greece and southern Greece. The Corinthians know nothing of what it cost you to bring the gospel to them."

A tear coursed down Paul's face.

"I have struggled with this. Perhaps, yes, for their sakes, I should say a few words."

Still, it would take Paul five or six more pages before he finally bared his heart. What he finally said make up the most beautiful passages Paul ever penned.

We try to live in such a way that no one will be hindered from finding the Lord by the way we act, and so no one can find fault with our ministry. In everything we do we try to show that we are true ministers of God. We patiently endure troubles and hardships and calamities of every kind. We have been beaten, been put in jail, faced angry mobs, worked to exhaustion, endured sleepless nights, and gone without food. We have proved ourselves by our purity, our understanding, our patience, our kindness, our sincere love, and the power of the Holy Spirit. We have faithfully preached the truth. God's power has been working in us. We have righteousness as our weapon, both to attack and to defend ourselves. We serve God whether people honor us or despise us, whether they slander us or praise us. We are honest, but they call us impostors. We are well known, but we are treated as unknown. We live close to death, but here we are, still alive. We have been beaten within an inch of our lives. Our hearts ache, but we always have joy. We are poor, but we give spiritual riches to others. We own nothing, and yet we have everything.

Oh, dear Corinthian friends! We have spoken honestly with you. Our hearts are open to you. If there is a problem between us, it is not because of a lack of love on our part, but because you have withheld your love from us. I am talking now as I would to my own children. Open your hearts to us!

It was obvious to all in the room that Paul was very uncomfortable with what he was doing. Nevertheless, what he declared was declared with a touch of majesty.

Paul began to plead with the Corinthians to open their hearts to him so that he might return to them, but more than just to return, to be received the way he was received on his very first visit there.

Timothy interrupted and said, "Paul, you should return to the subject of Titus. A few moments ago you only alluded to the agony you went through when you discovered, in Troas, that

Titus was missing. You have left out much of the story of those awful days when you thought Titus was dead."

Paul looked over at Titus and replied: "Yes, when I arrived here in Philippi I was so certain you were dead, I had already *buried* you!"

We all laughed, none more than Titus.

"All right," said Paul, "the whole story!"

When we arrived in Macedonia there was no rest for us. Outside there was conflict from every direction, and inside there was fear. But God, who encourages those who are discouraged, encouraged us by the arrival of Titus. His presence was a joy, but so was the news he brought of the encouragement he received from you. When he told me how much you were looking forward to my visit, and how sorry you were about what had happened, and how loyal your love is for me, I was filled with joy!

I am no longer sorry that I sent that letter to you, though I was sorry for a time, for I know that it was painful to you for a little while. Now I am glad I sent it, not because it hurt you, but because the pain caused you to have remorse and change your ways. It was the kind of sorrow God wants his people to have, so you were not harmed by us in any way. For God can use sorrow in our lives to help us turn away from sin and seek salvation. We will never regret that kind of sorrow. But sorrow without repentance is the kind that results in death.

It was a wonder that Tertius could keep up with Paul, for at this time Paul had broken loose with wonderful words of rejoicing over the way Corinth had received Titus.

Titus was quite obviously touched as he heard Paul recount the positive side of this story.

We were especially delighted to see how happy Titus was at the way you welcomed him and set his mind at ease. I had told him how proud I was of you—and you didn't disappoint me. I have always told you the truth, and now my boasting to Titus has also proved true! Now he cares for you more than ever when he remembers the way you listened to him and welcomed him with such respect and deep concern. I am very happy now because I have complete confidence in you.

It was late afternoon. I, Priscilla, along with Lydia, slipped out of the room.

"I believe it is time our brother Paul took a rest," I said to her.

"My servants are preparing food," she responded. "I had already come to the conclusion that brother Paul would be at that letter all night. Let us see that he lays aside the letter long enough to add some strength to his body."

So it was that Lydia stepped back into Paul's room.

"Brother Paul," she said, speaking as only Lydia could, "there is food. Please come."

Paul had long ago learned to obey this woman. He stood.

"Brothers, some food. Then we will continue. The best, I have decided, will be saved for the last!"

CHAPTER 10

"It was several years ago when Peter and I spoke together about the drought in Israel," shared Paul, as we sat down to eat.

"The very first church I spoke to concerning a collection was the church in Corinth. They were so willing to help—at least they were at *that* time! I cannot but wonder if their hearts are still for this collection," he said grimly. "Titus, can you tell everyone here what Corinth's attitude is toward collecting money for Jerusalem . . . at *this* moment?"

"When I spoke to them about their previous plans to send money, they not only responded well—they actually *begged* me to allow them to send the money to their Jewish counterpart. They have been collecting money for a long time," said Titus.

"I am proud of them," responded Paul with obvious satisfaction. "When this meal is ended, I shall take up that very subject. Then, on to a few kind words about my Pharisaical friend."

It was with a great deal of expectation that we followed the indefatigable Paul back to his room. Eyes dancing, he rushed forward, Tertius in lock step with every word.

Now I want to tell you, dear brothers and sisters, what God in his kindness has done for the churches in Macedonia. Though they have been going through much trouble and hard times, their wonderful joy and deep poverty have overflowed in rich generosity.

(We immediately saw what Paul was doing. He was going to stir up the Corinthian church—in southern Greece—by telling them of the liberal giving of the churches in *northern* Greece.)

For I can testify that they gave not only what they could afford but far more. And they did it of their own free will. They begged us again and again for the gracious privilege of sharing in the gift for the Christians in Jerusalem. Best of all, they went beyond our highest hopes, for their first action was to dedicate themselves to the Lord and to us for whatever directions God might give them.

So we have urged Titus, who encouraged your giving in the first place, to return to you and encourage you to complete your share in this ministry of giving. Since you excel in so many ways—you have so much faith, such gifted speakers, such knowledge, such enthusiasm, and such love for us—now I want you to excel also in this gracious ministry of giving. I am not saying you must do it, even though the other churches are eager to do it. This is one way to prove your love is real.

You know how full of love and kindness our Lord Jesus Christ was. Though he was very rich, yet for your sakes he became poor, so that by his poverty he could make you rich.

I suggest that you finish what you started a year ago, for you were the first to propose this idea, and you were the first to begin doing something about it. Now you should carry this project through to completion just as enthusiastically as you began it. Give whatever you can according to what you have. If you are really eager to give, it isn't important how much you are able to give. God wants you to give what you have, not what you don't have. Of course, I don't mean you should give so much that you suffer from having too little. I only mean that there should be some equality. Right now you have plenty and can help them. Then at some other time they can share with you when you need it. In this way, everyone's needs will be met. Do you remember what the Scriptures say about this? "Those who gathered a lot had nothing left over, and those who gathered only a little had enough."

Paul paused the dictation and mused aloud, "Now I must tell Corinth that Titus will be returning to them."

"Are you going to do this *without* talking to Titus?" asked Timothy.

"I have already talked to him. He is itching to return to Corinth," said Paul, smiling.

"Oh," said Timothy, as he shoved at Titus.

"You are jealous!" said Titus, pulling himself back upright. "Just you remember, Timothy, that *you* were the very first person Paul *ever* sent out."

"Enough of this!" insisted Paul, waving them off.

"Tertius?"

"I am ready, though I confess, my hand is not quite so compliant."

I am thankful to God that he has given Titus the same enthusiasm for you that I have. He welcomed our request that he visit you again. In fact, he himself was eager to go and see you. We are also sending another brother with Titus. He is highly praised in all the churches as a preacher of the Good News. He was appointed by the churches to accompany us as we take the offering to Jerusalem—a service that glorifies the Lord and shows our eagerness to help. By traveling together we will guard against any suspicion, for we are anxious that no one should find fault with the way we are handling this generous gift. We are careful to be honorable before the Lord, but we also want everyone else to know we are honorable.

And we are also sending with them another brother who

has been thoroughly tested and has shown how earnest he is on many occasions. He is now even more enthusiastic because of his increased confidence in you. If anyone asks about Titus, say that he is my partner who works with me to help you. And these brothers are representatives of the churches. They are splendid examples of those who bring glory to Christ. So show them your love, and prove to all the churches that our boasting about you is justified.

Paul then did what he so often did in writing a letter: He returned to a former subject. This time he went back to the subject of *giving*.

I really don't need to write to you about this gift for the Christians in Jerusalem. For I know how eager you are to help, and I have been boasting to our friends in Macedonia that you Christians in Greece were ready to send an offering a year ago. In fact, it was your enthusiasm that stirred up many of them to begin helping.

At that, to my surprise, Paul told the Corinthians that he would not only be sending Titus back to Corinth but also Luke. Do you wonder at my surprise? Then let me explain.

Luke going with *Titus?* Everyone in the room either laughed or smiled upon hearing that Luke would be *assisting* Titus. There was good reason for our amusement. Try as he may, Luke never really felt comfortable believing that his young nephew Titus was as gifted and capable as the rest of us knew Titus to be. Now, here was Paul about to send Luke to *help* his nephew!

Sending Luke to help Titus would surely gall Luke. (I must remind you that just three years after that day, Luke began writing the history of the apostles and the churches that the apostles planted. Never once in that story of twenty-eight pages did Luke ever mention Titus.)

Paul ended his second reference to giving with these words:

You will be glorifying God through your generous gifts. For your generosity to [the Christians in Jerusalem] will prove that you are obedient to the Good News of Christ. And they will pray for you with deep affection because of the wonderful grace of God shown through you.

Thank God for his Son—a gift too wonderful for words!

There was obviously a great passion in Paul's heart for the poor in Jerusalem, but he had a secondary reason for collecting money for them. Nor was this something he tried to keep secret. Turmoil was growing in Israel. Feelings against the Romans were running high throughout all of Israel. Rumors of rebellion were everywhere. This anti-Roman attitude had somehow spilled over to criticism of all *Gentile* believers!

Some Jews still could not abide the idea of Gentile *churches*, especially ones raised up by Paul. Many still believed that the idea of the uncircumcised believing in the Messiah was equal to blasphemy.

Paul knew a large gift to the Jerusalem poor—from Gentile believers—would impress even the most skeptical resident of Jerusalem.

Somehow we all sensed that Paul was about to charge into a new topic. Knowing this, Timothy took the opportunity to interrupt Paul.

He said, "Brother, when you do arrive in Corinth, there are going to be a few in the ecclesia there who will oppose you. Probably they will do no more than sit in silence with a disgruntled look on their faces; nonetheless, I implore you, be more direct in writing about your apostleship. They *all* need to hear about the authority that the Lord has given you. Again, Paul, the *entire* story. Please."

Titus voiced his agreement: "Granted, you have said more

personal things in this letter than ever before. However, I join in asking you to let the brothers and sisters in Corinth know the suffering you passed through in Galatia, northern Greece, and Asia Minor—*and* do not forget Cyprus."

"Or Syria," enjoined Timothy.

"I would feel foolish to do so," responded Paul quietly.

"Then be foolish!" replied Titus emphatically.

Paul was a very strong-willed man. I, Priscilla, suppose that he had to be strong-willed because of all that he had to endure during his sojourn on this earth. But I have also watched Paul yield so many, many times to brothers on occasions when they have spoken to him in no uncertain terms. And *that* is exactly what Titus had done.

It was almost midnight. Still, Paul was determined to finish the letter.

"All right. A fool I shall be!" he declared.

"Wonderful!" I clapped.

With that, Paul began that marvelous defense of his life and his ministry. "I have been sent by the Lord to raise up assemblies among the Gentiles," he murmured just before he threw himself into his defense.

> Now I, Paul, plead with you. I plead with the gentleness and kindness that Christ himself would use, even though some of you say I am bold in my letters but timid in person.

As it has often been said, the greatest issue Paul and his coworkers ever faced was found in the question "Who is Paul?"

He was attacked so much, by so many, that many Gentiles left their assemblies because they had come to distrust the ever-attacked Paul. But, remember, they did so only on the grounds of what they had *heard* that was said against him, *not* what they saw.

Paul was the issue. He was *always* the issue. The words I

remember most about Paul are these, which he himself spoke: "I am an aroma of death to some, and an aroma of life to others."

After Paul was beheaded in Rome, the young men who took his place soon faced the very same issue. Over and again people asked them, "Who is Timothy? Who is Titus? Who is Aristarchus? Who is Sopater? Who is Gaius? By what authority do these men do these things? By what authority do they speak?"

This was never an issue among the Twelve. *Jesus* himself had chosen them. *Jesus* had trained them *and* sent them out. But concerning Paul and the Eight, controversy surrounded them all . . . for as long as they lived. (That controversy continues until this very hour, and it will probably continue for several more generations.)

It was there in Lydia's home that Paul finally, after twenty years of being a follower of Christ, responded to his critics—and he did so with a resounding declaration.

(I, Priscilla, would hope that every person who has ever heard of this Paul of Tarsus would seek out this letter to Corinth, find this passage, and read what our brother Paul wrote. Let those who criticize him, or the Eight, know who this man is.)

So began the very heart of Paul's recitation of his sufferings and triumphs.

> I hope you will be patient with me as I keep on talking like a fool. Please bear with me. I am jealous for you with the jealousy of God himself. For I promised you as a pure bride to one husband, Christ. But I fear that somehow you will be led away from your pure and simple devotion to Christ, just as Eve was deceived by the serpent. You seem to believe whatever anyone tells you, even if they preach about a different Jesus than the one we preach, or a different Spirit than the one you received, or a different kind of gospel than the one you believed. But I don't think I am inferior to these "super

apostles." I may not be a trained speaker, but I know what I am talking about. I think you realize this by now, for we have proved it again and again.

Did I do wrong when I humbled myself and honored you by preaching God's Good News to you without expecting anything in return? I "robbed" other churches by accepting their contributions so I could serve you at no cost. And when I was with you and didn't have enough to live on, I did not ask you to help me. For the brothers who came from Macedonia brought me another gift. I have never yet asked you for any support, and I never will. As surely as the truth of Christ is in me, I will never stop boasting about this all over Greece. Why? Because I don't love you? God knows I do.

But I will continue doing this to cut the ground out from under the feet of those who boast that their work is just like ours. These people are false apostles. They have fooled you by disguising themselves as apostles of Christ. But I am not surprised! Even Satan can disguise himself as an angel of light. So it is no wonder his servants can also do it by pretending to be godly ministers. In the end they will get every bit of punishment their wicked deeds deserve.

Once again, don't think that I have lost my wits to talk like this. But even if you do, listen to me, as you would to a foolish person, while I also boast a little. Such bragging is not something the Lord wants, but I am acting like a fool. And since others boast about their human achievements, I will, too. After all, you, who think you are so wise, enjoy listening to fools! You put up with it when they make you their slaves, take everything you have, take advantage of you, put on airs, and slap you in the face. I'm ashamed to say that we were not strong enough to do that!

But whatever they dare to boast about—I'm talking like

a fool again—I can boast about it, too. They say they are Hebrews, do they? So am I. And they say they are Israelites? So am I. And they are descendants of Abraham? So am I. They say they serve Christ? I know I sound like a madman, but I have served him far more! I have worked harder, been put in jail more often, been whipped times without number, and faced death again and again. Five different times the Jews gave me thirty-nine lashes. Three times I was beaten with rods. Once I was stoned. Three times I was shipwrecked. Once I spent a whole night and a day adrift at sea. I have traveled many weary miles. I have faced danger from flooded rivers and from robbers. I have faced danger from my own people, the Jews, as well as from the Gentiles. I have faced danger in the cities, in the deserts, and on the stormy seas. And I have faced danger from men who claim to be Christians but are not. I have lived with weariness and pain and sleepless nights. Often I have been hungry and thirsty and have gone without food. Often I have shivered with cold, without enough clothing to keep me warm.

Then, besides all this, I have the daily burden of how the churches are getting along. Who is weak without my feeling that weakness? Who is led astray, and I do not burn with anger?

If I must boast, I would rather boast about the things that show how weak I am. God, the Father of our Lord Jesus, who is to be praised forever, knows I tell the truth. When I was in Damascus, the governor under King Aretas kept guards at the city gates to catch me. But I was lowered in a basket through a window in the city wall, and that's how I got away!

All who sat in that room were spellbound. I hardly dared breath. Tears were pouring down my face. My husband was in a similar state. Lydia was unrestrained in her weeping. At last we heard from Paul's own lips what he had suffered in all those places where he had raised up churches.

Paul asked for some water. Still no one spoke. It was only for a moment that Paul sipped the water. Eyes filled with tears, he continued to tell his story:

This boasting is all so foolish, but let me go on.

Paul had cut loose from all the moorings he had placed on his testimony. There, in the middle of the night, Paul revealed much of himself that *no one* had ever heard before. I was quite sure the Corinthians would be as astounded as we were.

Let me tell about the visions and revelations I received from the Lord. I was caught up into the third heaven fourteen years ago. Whether my body was there or just my spirit, I don't know; only God knows. But I do know that I was caught up into paradise and heard things so astounding that they cannot be told. That experience is something worth boasting about, but I am not going to do it. I am going to boast only about my weaknesses.

Paul looked around the room. He said to us, "I dare not stop here. I am not particularly proud of what I have just said. My weaknesses are far greater than my strengths—God knows that. But because I am weak, God has made me weaker. Further, in the places where I am strong, God has broken me. He has done this by many, many means. But there is a man, a man whom God sent into my life who has done more to break me, to cause me to yield up to loss, to embrace failure, than everyone and everything else combined."

I put my hand over my mouth. I knew without a doubt that Paul was not only going to break his silence concerning Blastinius, but that he would turn it all to the glory of God.

Paul began to choke. In fact, he could hardly breathe. Suddenly, Paul grabbed his side. It was not the first time. On several occasions, when faced with the destruction wrought upon his ministry by Blastinius, Paul had grasped his side.

A moment passed; Paul straightened and, to our dismay, went on more intent than ever.

"The greatest boast I have in all the world," he declared with a strong voice, "is that *God* sent Blastinius Drachrachma into my life."

What Paul said next were words that everyone in Corinth would clearly understand. *They* had *met* Blastinius. They had seen him going about, in Corinth, doing his insidious task of destroying Paul. They had even met Blastinius's cohorts *in* the Corinthian gatherings. They had witnessed just how ruthlessly those men cut at Paul's reputation.

And so . . . for the first and only time . . . Paul openly addressed the matter of his great enemy. Yet, bless his memory, even here Paul never actually mentioned Blastinius's name.

> I have plenty to boast about and would be no fool in doing it, because I would be telling the truth. But I won't do it. I don't want anyone to think more highly of me than what they can actually see in my life and my message, even though I have received wonderful revelations from God. But to keep me from getting puffed up, I was given a thorn in my flesh, a messenger from Satan to torment me and keep me from getting proud.
>
> Three different times I begged the Lord to take it away. Each time he said, "My gracious favor is all you need. My power works best in your weakness." So now I am glad to boast about my weaknesses, so that the power of Christ may work through me. Since I know it is all for Christ's good, I am quite content with my weaknesses and with insults, hardships, persecutions, and calamities. For when I am weak, then I am strong.

You have made me act like a fool—boasting like this. You ought to be writing commendations for me, for I am not at all inferior to these "super apostles," even though I am nothing at all. When I was with you, I certainly gave you every proof that I am truly an apostle, sent to you by God himself. For I patiently did many signs and wonders and miracles among you. The only thing I didn't do, which I do in the other churches, was to become a burden to you. Please forgive me for this wrong!

"Incredible," stammered Timothy, searching for words to match his emotions.

"Blastinius was right; you really can write heavy letters," sighed Titus, falling back against the wall.

Paul raised his hand, letting us know he had something he wanted to announce: "Titus, you have been eager to return to Corinth. Thank you for such bold willingness. You will deliver this letter to Corinth. As I have already said, *Luke* will accompany you. After this letter is read, report back to me immediately."

"Are you sure about Luke? He does not hold me in very high regard. To him I will always be a little kid running around in the streets of Antioch with a runny nose."

"Yes, Luke will go with you," replied Paul softly, yet emphatically. "Further, if Corinth survives *this* letter, I will come to them. But tell the Corinthians I cannot stay long—perhaps no more than three months. Then I must turn back north toward Berea and Thessalonica.

"Oh," he exclaimed, "before any of that happens, I will visit one other place . . . a place unknown to any of you."

Paul had done it again! He loved to be mysterious, reveling in surprises. Of course we all wanted to ask where *that* place was, yet knew full well he would not tell us. At least not now.

Titus was the wise one. "*When* will you tell us where this place is?"

"Soon enough!" said Paul. "Now, Tertius, if you have sufficient ink, let us go on."

Now I am coming to you for the third time, and I will not be a burden to you. I don't want what you have; I want you. And anyway, little children don't pay for their parents' food. It's the other way around; parents supply food for their children. I will gladly spend myself and all I have for your spiritual good, even though it seems that the more I love you, the less you love me.

Some of you admit I was not a burden to you. But they still think I was sneaky and took advantage of you by trickery. But how? Did any of the men I sent to you take advantage of you?

Paul looked up. "Titus, did you take any money while you were in Corinth?"

"I did not," growled Titus.

"Good! Then I can continue."

When I urged Titus to visit you and sent our other brother with him, did Titus take advantage of you? No, of course not! For we both have the same Spirit and walk in each other's steps, doing things the same way.

Paul then grumbled something under his breath that we could not understand. Tertius picked up his pen and glanced at Paul who said, "It is late. No, it is now *early;* the sun will soon rise. Shall we continue?"

"Yes," said Tertius, rising to the challenge.

Perhaps you think we are saying all this just to defend ourselves. That isn't it at all. We tell you this as Christ's servants, and we know that God is listening. Everything we do, dear friends, is for your benefit. For I am afraid that when I come to visit you I won't like what I find, and then you won't like my response. I am afraid that I will find quarreling, jealousy, outbursts of anger, selfishness, backstabbing, gossip, conceit, and disorderly behavior. Yes, I am afraid that when I come, God will humble me again because of you.

Paul added a few more stern words, aimed straight at those who doubted his authority, his calling, his sending; but most of all, he shot strong words like arrows at those who spoke of him as being weak.

It may surprise you to hear that I have always seen Paul as a very humble man. Many failed to realize that fact, because he was ... well ... quite self-assured. Nonetheless, I knew what he meant by "weak."

"Weak" may be contrary to the impression of those who have never met Paul. The impression of Paul's being strong stems mostly from the fact that he was so very controversial. But the Paul we know is a man who would lose and lose again—a man who was loath to correct, a man who would willingly suffer defeat, time after time, with those defeats coming into his life only because he was unwilling to defend himself. Yes, he was self-assured. He had met the Lord face-to-face. He knew he was called ... *and* sent. A man could find self-confidence as a result of this fact! Still he was the most humble man any of us ever knew. Strong beyond words, yet weak where God wants weakness.

We are glad to be weak, if you are really strong. What we pray for is your restoration to maturity.

I am writing this to you before I come, hoping that I won't need to deal harshly with you when I do come. For I want to use the authority the Lord has given me to build you up, not to tear you down.

Paul leaned back and closed his eyes. He had finished—finished a most remarkable and revealing letter.

"Please write these closing words, Tertius," continued Paul without opening his eyes. Tears once more flowed down Paul's face. There were even tears in the eyes of Tertius.

> Dear brothers and sisters, I close my letter with these last words: Rejoice. Change your ways. Encourage each other. Live in harmony and peace. Then the God of love and peace will be with you.
>
> Greet each other in Christian love. All the Christians here send you their greetings.
>
> May the grace of our Lord Jesus Christ, the love of God, and the fellowship of the Holy Spirit be with you all.

It was almost morning.

Rousing himself Paul said, "Priscilla, Aquila: I believe we are near the time you should leave Philippi and continue on your journey to Rome . . . along with our five thunderbolts from Galatia. You have made it safely from Ephesus to Philippi. May God now speed you on safely to Rome.

"May I suggest you begin searching out the best caravan or Roman garrison that is traversing the Greek peninsula on its way to the Adriatic Sea. There will be, let's see . . . eight of you. Are you sure you three civilized people can endure the five Galatians?"

"It will be our honor," replied Aquila. "And if they get out of hand, I will turn them over to Epenetus."

"Why?" I asked. "He is just like one of them . . . an over-enthusiastic single brother."

Paul turned to Titus and Timothy. "When you and I have finished reviewing Tertius's final draft of this letter, and when several copies have been made, it will be time for you, Titus, to head south for Corinth. Soon after Priscilla's party heads for

Rome, and you go to Corinth, and the forty all arrive, *then* I will set out for Corinth.

"Titus, you and Luke please be clear in telling the Corinthians that I cannot come to them until all the brothers and sisters who are destined for Rome arrive here in Philippi. Then, once they are all safely on their way to Rome, I *will* come to Corinth."

"How long do you expect to be here before you come to Corinth? They will ask, you know," replied Titus.

Thoughtfully, Paul turned the question over in his mind.

"I have been here less than a week. Everyone going to Rome has been told to come to Philippi first. Let's see . . . they should all be here within the next three or four weeks. I plan to accompany them to the Greek port of Dyrrhachium. And then . . .

"I would venture it will take us about two weeks to cross overland from Philippi to Dyrrhachium. After seeing everyone on board ship to Rome, I will then—most likely—turn south for Corinth. Tell the Corinthians to expect me in *about* three months, and that I expect to be there with them three months."

Paul then greeted the dawn with a prayer.

A few days later Epenetus, Aquila, five young brothers from Galatia, and I set forth for Rome. Titus and Luke turned south for Corinth.

And, just as Paul had surmised, Lydia's house soon began to fill with brothers and sisters arriving from all over the empire.

That is a story in itself.

CHAPTER 11

Where route did I take to get to Rome? I traveled with Epenetus, Aquila, and the five Galatian brothers (Asyncritus, Phlegon, Hermes, Patrobas, and Hermas). We joined a Roman garrison in Philippi headed west for Dyrrhachium. We then took a ship that crossed the Adriatic Sea, docking at Brundisium, Italy. We still had four hundred more miles to walk before we reached Rome. Some of the men were concerned that I might not be up to such a long journey. Before we reached Rome, I was the one concerned about them!

While we were doing this, those forty other brothers and sisters were converging on Philippi. Lydia later wrote to me: "You have only *five* overenthusiastic saints. I have *forty* such people to contend with. But never mind, I am sending them *all* to you. Perhaps it would be wise to notify all of Rome that they are coming. One thing is certain: Rome will never be the same again."

After all forty saints had arrived in Philippi, Paul spent several days talking with them about history, Italy, Rome, and their purpose for going to the Imperial city.

Who were these forty people?

First, there were Paul's kin, Andronicus and Junia, Jews

from Jerusalem. Then there was Ampliatus, a recently freed slave. Then there were a number of men from Asia Minor who worked for an empirewide company owned by a wealthy merchant named Aristobulus. Another of Paul's kin, Herodion, had formerly been a servant in a company owned by Herod's family.

Another group of young men came from Syria. They worked for the worldwide trading company that had formerly been owned by the famous and rich Narcissus. (His organization had been seized by the emperor.) Then there were Tryphena and Tryphosa, twin sisters from southern Greece. Persis, from Antioch, as well as Rufus, of Antioch, the son of Simon who carried the Lord's cross on the day he was crucified. Rufus brought his mother along with him. She had insisted that if Paul made it to Rome, *she* would cook Paul's meals and see after his needs, just as she had always done for him when he was in Antioch.

There was a young married couple, Philologus and his wife, Julia. Nereus and his sister, as well as a sister called Olympas, all who had sailed together from Asia Minor to Philippi. These brought with them several servants, also believers.

There were also Urbanus (large in spiritual stature but small in physical stature) and Stachys, both from Cyprus.

That is a sampling. Altogether there were about forty believers, plus the five from Galatia.

Once these believers arrived in Philippi, they spent a great deal of time together with Paul in prayer, fervent prayer.

The day came for them to depart Philippi. Paul walked with them all the way to Dyrrhachium, a port on the west coast of Greece. The garrison of soldiers with whom they walked had never beheld people with so much joy, singing, laughing, and hugging. After ten days of walking, the company of over fifty reached Dyrrhachium. It was there that Paul revealed his surprise.

"There is a new Roman road being built north of here, following along the Adriatic Sea. The road leads to a land called Dalmatia. When that road is finished, men will be able to walk north along the Adriatic Sea to a point that parallels Rome. Perhaps one day we will sail not from Dyrrhachium but from Dalmatia. This will mean men can walk across the Italian peninsula from the east side of Italy, due west, to Rome."

Paul continued, "I want to see this land. I want to stand there and dream of sailing from Dalmatia to Italy . . . and on to Rome.

"Once everyone is safely aboard a ship bound for Italy, I plan to walk upon the western side of the Greek shoreline until I come to Dalmatia."

"So that is the 'other place' you plan to visit," said Gaius.

"Exactly," said Paul. "And I hope, one day, to see a church raised up in that land."

At that point Aquila took Paul aside.

"Brother Paul, the population of Rome is of every race and kin. Rome has few Romans in it! So many brothers and sisters already know Christ, and they know the life of the body—the assembly is bound to grow very fast. And, yes, she will be a strong assembly, but many new believers will be added who will know little of Christ and even less about life in the ecclesia. I urge you to write the assembly in Rome just as soon as it is born.

"If you do, address all the facets of our faith. The Jew, the Gentile, our place in Christ, suffering, triumph. And, most of all, write to those of us gathering in Rome about *how* to live with one another in peace in the church. Make that part of the letter very *practical*. Speak to the new converts *and* to us older converts! Make it a glorious letter. Give us the very measure of our faith. We will then see to it that every new believer who becomes part of us will either read that letter or hear it read. Who knows, perhaps we may be able to use such a letter for another ten or fifteen years, always reading it to those who have just believed in Christ. If you do this, do not forget to add some encouraging words . . . about *the cross*. The cross which each of us must bear."

Paul's eyes glistened, his face lifted. "An excellent idea, one worthy of serious consideration."

Paul wrote that letter just a few months later. In fact, I, Priscilla, was the first person in Italy to read that letter! I had no idea how inspiring that letter would be, nor its impact on our lives. (Even today, many years after all these events, copies of the letter are being passed out all over the empire.)

So it came about that some forty believers set sail for "the heel on the boot" of Italy. From there, following the route I had taken a few weeks earlier, they walked four hundred miles up the Italian peninsula to Rome. What a day it was when all those people came trooping into my home on Aventine Hill.

Having watched their ship sail out of the Dyrrhachium harbor, Paul made plans to turn north and visit the land of Illyricum and Dalmatia. There in Dyrrhachium, Paul announced to his young friends, "I am going to Dalmatia. You men will stay here and bring Christ to Dyrrhachium."

An immediate protest arose. The seven men were thrilled at the thought of all of them proclaiming Christ in one city—a city where Christ was unknown; but they found unacceptable the thought of leaving Paul to journey alone, on an unfinished road, up into the wild land of Dalmatia. Protestation was loud, wills unbending. Finally there was a compromise. Six men would remain in Dyrrhachium. Who would go with Paul? The issue was settled by the casting of lots. The toss fell to Gaius.

It was a providential choice. Gaius, bold, aggressive, and fearless, could, to a degree, even stand up to Paul.

Paul had set out to see a land few knew anything about, except for rumors: "The Dalmatians are a wild people in a beautiful but wild land."

CHAPTER 12

Throughout their northern trek, Paul and Gaius were never out of sight of soldiers, slaves, and architects, busy laying a road that one day was supposed to reach all the way to the town of Scodra. Upon arriving in Dalmatia, Paul encountered a vivacious, indomitable people, who, in their appearance, managed to be at once both dark-headed *and* sandy-headed. Paul and Gaius succeeded in preaching the gospel in Dalmatia but faced an insurmountable language problem. Only a few responded to their message.

"Someone, someday, must return here," Paul repeated again and again as he and Gaius turned back to Dyrrhachium.

(Dalmatia marked the northernmost and westernmost place Paul had ever reached, until he went to Rome some three years later.)

In the meantime, the six (Sopater, Secundus, Timothy, Aristarchus, Tychicus, and Trophimus) had met with great success. In the month they were there another church had been added to the number of assemblies in Greece. The number of people who gathered in Dyrrhachium was small, but their conversions were real. Seeing this, Paul immediately dispatched a letter to Philippi asking that brothers in the assembly there come quickly to Dyrrhachium to assist these new believers.

At last Paul was now free to turn south, to Titus, to Luke, and to the ecclesia in Corinth.

Would Paul be accepted in the church in Corinth? If so, just *how* welcome? Or did that letter cause problems like the earlier letter had? What had transpired in the minds of the Corinthians since Titus had returned there? A ship in the seaport of Dyrrhachium, bound for the western port of Corinth, would soon give Paul his answers.

As he and his friends boarded the ship, Paul asked: "Shall this journey to Corinth be in triumph or in vain? It can be only one of the two."

I will now tell you what happened there in Corinth exactly as Timothy related it to me.

Timothy, you and the others go on into Corinth tonight. I will remain here, outside the walls, until daybreak. Tomorrow, return to me—tell me if the saints in Corinth are *really* willing to receive me. I will not enter Corinth if I am not welcome," said Paul, resigned.

That night Paul had much to consider.

"I am so controversial—everywhere. God's people can take just so much confusion and controversy about me, or *anyone*. Even if they believe in me, that is one thing, but can they keep receiving me, knowing that to follow Paul is to live in a storm? Welcome I may be, but my effectiveness rests upon more than that. People do not willingly walk straight into a storm, and I *am* a storm."

Paul kept an anxious vigil that evening, hoping the morrow would bring better news than he was capable of imagining. But even before dawn, Gaius returned.

"Paul, the Daggermen are on their way back to Corinth! We are *certain* they are coming here . . . and, once more, they are looking for *you*. They *know* you are coming."

"Hmmm, the Daggermen have sought me in several cities, but it turned out I was never there," replied Paul. "This time . . . ?"

"It is important that from now on you keep your head low," responded a very concerned Gaius.

"*Keep my head low!* I have never heard that phrase. Is that some sort of saying you have in Galatia?"

"Yes, it is. We say, 'Keep your head low, your face down, and be one who has no name.' "

"Good advice. If I enter Corinth, I will follow your wise words. Now, when do the Daggermen arrive?"

"We have only been assured that they are on their way."

"So it has come to this," mused Paul. "The *sicarii* have vowed to kill Peter *and* me. Neither of us has done anything except proclaim Israel's Messiah. The world seems to be determined not only to kill our Lord but to end the lives of those who announce him."

"I was sent to stay with you through the rest of the night. I will sit against the door. You sleep."

Paul eyed Gaius closely, then decided a protest was not worth the energy. "All right, to sleep! *Both* of us!"

The next morning, at sunup, Titus and Timothy arrived.

"Give your name!" said Gaius roughly.

"I am an uncircumcised Syrian, come to make war on the Gauls," responded Titus.

"Oh," replied Gaius, "then I have nothing to fear. Come in, Syrian, and meet your sure demise!"

Timothy took up the lightheartedness of the moment: "Marked for death are you, Paul? Well, at least you will die in the midst of a small handful of Corinthians who love you!"

Paul sat up and said: "Am I to take those last words literally?"

"On the contrary! The number of believers in the church in Corinth who are eagerly looking forward to receiving you, without qualification, is overwhelming," said Titus.

"But not all?" responded Paul.

"Paul, there has never been a day in your life when *everybody* was willing to receive you."

"I suppose I am satisfied with the *overwhelming majority*," said Paul.

In the laughter that followed Paul finally admitted to himself that he was loved in Corinth.

Titus continued: "You owe a great deal of your acceptance to one Blastinius Drachrachma! They had heard of him or met him, or his cohorts. Now—at last—they know of the mischief he caused in Antioch, the deep problems he created in Galatia, the rumors he has spread about you, everywhere. They also know he has stirred up the Daggermen against you. They have also heard of Blastinius's letters that he sent to synagogues all over Asia Minor. And Greece. As to his cohorts, the minute they entered the Corinthian assembly the Lord's people saw right through them.

"That later letter also helped. Many cried when they heard it read aloud to the assemblies. And, as the letter was being read, *everyone* knew exactly *who* your *thorn* was.

"Blastinius has stabbed himself with his own sword!" said Titus, grinning.

"The brothers and sisters were insistent on coming out to see you, but I was just as insistent that they receive you only at night. The time and the place for the meeting have not yet been designated: We will wait until the very last minute.

"The *sicarii* may or may not have arrived, but the entire empire seems to know they are on their way here."

"The ecclesia *is* willing to receive me, even though I am marked for death?" asked Paul.

"With open arms, my brother," answered Titus.

At that moment Sopater came to the door.

"Please enter," said Gaius. "But know that if you had been any other Jew, I would have searched you for daggers."

"If I had one, it would have your name on it," gibed

Sopater, whose Jewish lineage was so small a part of his life, few of us ever even remembered he was Jewish.

"Sit down, all of you," scolded Paul. "Timothy, you were with me the first time my feet ever trod this city. You have returned here several times. Titus, you have been here twice, and the last time you were here for several months. Between the two of you, you should be able to give me an idea of the entire situation I am about to face."

For over three hours the five men talked. Finally, Paul reached a conclusion: "I will enter Corinth. I will remain here several months and strengthen the church. I will prepare them for an uncertain future. I will minister to them as though this were my last visit." An indefinite smile crossed Paul's face. "It very well may be!" he said.

"What of the Daggermen?" asked Timothy.

Paul quickly responded, "I will keep my head low, my face down, and be as a man who has no name."

"Paul, I do not think that you should go to Jerusalem," said Timothy, ignoring Paul's quotation of the Galatian saying.

Paul jerked his head around toward Timothy. "What, and miss watching you eight brothers walk the streets of Jerusalem? And you would have no one to answer your questions!"

"We are more interested in the *new* Jerusalem," said Gaius. "It is not necessary for us to see Jerusalem. The money for the poor can arrive by other men, or we can go without you. Timothy can introduce us to the city—you need not be there."

"No, I must go to Jerusalem. We are on the verge of a very serious rift between the Gentile churches and the Jewish assemblies. This rift must never happen. I will gladly risk my life to see a restoring of the bond between the Jewish and Greek believers. I know I speak for Peter as well. He is just as determined that the Hebrew churches and the Gentile churches must be one. Peter would do no less than I will do."

"Paul, I think I can honestly say that at this moment you are the most talked about person in Israel, Galatia, and Asia Minor. Perhaps, other than Nero, the most talked about man in the empire."

"Do not flatter me with such words. Quite frankly, I am pleased to know that I am on the tongues of men in Israel, and Asia Minor. This may fall out to the furtherance of the gospel."

"*And* to your funeral!" responded Gaius.

Paul's next words had nothing to do with the subject at hand. "I want someone to send a message to Tertius in Philippi."

"To Tertius?" asked Timothy.

"Yes. Andronicus, who is even now on his way to Rome, has urged me to write a letter to the fellowship of believers who are beginning to meet in Priscilla's house on Aventine Hill.

"I plan to write a letter to the Roman assembly. I will do so while I am here in Corinth. That letter needs to be sent to Rome in two languages: one in Latin, one in Greek. Tertius is the one person who can do that with complete precision."

"So sad, Timothy, you have been replaced," said Titus.

"You noticed my tears?"

Ignoring them, Paul went on: "This letter will be unlike anything I have previously written. It will be a letter covering the entire scope of our faith. Perhaps it can be used by the church in Rome for several years to come. The new believers, especially, will be helped by it at the time they join themselves to the Roman assembly."

"It appears your past letters are being copied and sent out to many places. Even your letter to Corinth, so recently written, is already being copied and passed on to the other assemblies in Greece. But even more so, your letter to the Galatians. *That* letter is being passed out *everywhere*," Titus informed him.

Paul looked honestly surprised. "I had no idea," he said blankly.

"I have further news for you. It has to do with that uncle of mine," said Titus.

Although he had no idea what was coming next, Paul laughed warmly. "You two have had a falling out?"

"Of course not. I respect the elderly!" retorted Titus.

"I am not sure what is going on between them," interrupted Timothy. "I spent some time with Luke last night. I think he is softening toward Titus. With a little time he might even be willing to admit that he has a nephew. Why, I could even believe that—given even more time—he might one day come to respect this uncircumcised heathen."

"Never!" responded Titus, with mock disbelief.

"Then what is your news?" Paul queried gruffly.

"Luke has become somewhat of a nuisance here," answered Titus. "He is talking to absolutely everyone about everything that happened to you in Greece. There is no end to his questions. Luke has done this before in other places—in Antioch and then in Philippi. He has come to know more about you and your travels than you do," continued Titus.

"But that is not all to tell," inserted Timothy again. "Wait until you hear what is going on with John Mark. He has done what Titus has been urging him to do for years: Mark is writing a short biography of the life of the Lord."

"Hallelujah!" said Paul, thrusting both hands into the air. "Praise God! I had feared that Peter and the other sent ones were going to pass on without having recorded anything permanent about the Lord's life. We need much more than oral tradition. This is wonderful news indeed. If there is any way to lay hold of Mark's works, we must make copies and send them to all the Gentile churches."

"There is more," continued Timothy; "It seems that Levi ..."

"You mean Matthew?" asked Paul.

"Yes, Matthew! It seems that Matthew read the story of the Lord's life by Mark. He felt it had one very great lacking—it did not include the Lord's genealogy."

"This is understandable," replied Paul. "There is a tradition among the Jews that when the Messiah comes, he will be able to announce his genealogy, not only back to David, but even back to Abraham."

Paul thought a moment. "If he is writing the Lord's genealogy, my guess is that Matthew will also include the Lord's birth. So many people think that Jesus is from Nazareth. So few are aware that he was born in Bethlehem, the very place where David was born. Excellent! God be with you, Matthew!

"Have either one of you seen these books, or are these rumors?"

"A copy of what Mark wrote is supposed to reach Corinth soon. As to Matthew's account, we have only heard rumors," said Titus.

Paul relaxed into a moment of quiet joy. "This is all good, but . . ."

"But what?" asked Titus.

"Both of those stories . . . ," said Paul, slowly and thoughtfully, "if we never have anything else, that will be good enough, but both are by Jews. I have a notion both books are addressed to Jews. It would be of great worth if someday the story of the Lord's life would be told from the viewpoint of a . . ." Paul's thoughts wandered off.

Suddenly Paul said, "It is getting late. Let us enter Corinth. Yes! At long last, Corinth!"

"We have some clothes here for you to put on, Paul."

"What!" said Paul, already protesting. Then, looking at the garment held out to him, he responded: "This is not the kind of clothing I wear."

"Exactly," said Timothy, "but it is the kind of clothing you are *going* to wear."

"To keep my head low, my face down, and remain nameless."

Timothy continued his instructions, "Not only are *we* expecting you to comply by putting on these clothes, but the church in Corinth is also expecting you to wear them!

"Further, you will move about only when surrounded by *us*. You will speak only at night, and you will leave before the meeting ends. If anyone follows you, the brothers in the church will follow *him*. You will not become an open mark for the *sicarii*."

Paul sighed. "Is my life really of such value? I doubt anyone will recall my name six months after I am dead."

"I will," replied Gaius, "but only because I will be remembering your stubbornness."

"Oh," remonstrated Paul. "And I have always expected to outlive you because of your foolhardiness!"

Paul then donned the most Gentile-looking clothes ever to cover his body.

"I disown you, Paul," teased Sopater. "I would never have anything to do with a Jew who looked so much the Gentile!"

At that, the five men set out for the center of Corinth.

The gathering that night was not only wonderful, but one of the most memorable hours of Paul's life.

C H A P T E R 1 4

The meeting was held in one of the largest halls in Corinth. The room filled long before the meeting began. Latecomers stood outside. When Paul stepped into the torch-lit room, the brothers and sisters immediately stood and began singing the poem of love that Paul had written in his first letter to them.

Paul began to cry. He had a capacity, once he started, to shed tears in a way very few men did. Spontaneously, everyone pressed in on him. The words they sang fit so beautifully. The room was filled with a sense of healing. Even Paul's most skeptical detractors were touched. Several of them pushed their way towards Paul and embraced him. Words of encouragement followed. So did repentance . . . and forgiveness.

The gathering in Corinth was a polyglot: Jews and Gentiles, with people of all languages, tribes, and cultures. The brotherhood there had never been strong . . . until that night.

Corinth had, at last, touched oneness.

When Paul stood to speak, he picked up exactly where he had left off at the time of his last departure. When he finished, questions began to fly. Several asked about that third shipwreck, as everyone had already heard the details of those two previous shipwrecks he had experienced.

But Paul found it too difficult to recount that story. All he could do was tell where the wreck took place and then add: "I was one of only three who survived—and that by God's mercy alone."

He then added: "I hope, by God's grace, there will never be another such shipwreck in my life." (Unfortunately, there would be a *fourth*, the worst of all.)

Someone in the room then dared bring up Blastinius. It was a name Paul almost never pronounced and one he virtually never heard. He chilled with the knowledge that the Corinthians even knew Blastinius Drachrachma's name.

"Let us never bother to speak of him," replied Paul. "His deeds are not worthy of our time, our thoughts, nor our discussion."

Nonetheless, one of the Jewish brothers, noted for being quite legalistic, responded: "Paul, I just recently read your letter to the *Galatians* . . . ."

"Oh no!" moaned Paul.

"Yes, a few copies of it have reached Corinth. Actually, Paul, it is a very beautiful letter. I mark the reading of that letter as a turning point in my life. Soon after I read it, the man you do not wish to speak of actually arrived here. It was as though the reading of your latest letter to us caused the man to suddenly come into existence. There among us stood the greatest legalist who ever lived! Even greater than *me!*"

Everyone in the room laughed until it hurt.

As the brother spoke, confessing his shame at his own legal attitudes, he kept repeating, "I saw myself in that man. I saw myself! I had to see Blastinius before I could ever see myself. What a law-centered man I have been. I have *never* really known freedom, nor grace.

"I learned so much from your Galatian letter. Yet I learned even more from Blastinius. I saw what it is to lose all one's freedom in Christ. I have been living the letter of the law while knowing nothing of the spirit. Blastinius and I are men who believe we can please God by carrying out a long list of do's and don'ts." The brother then cried out with a loud voice: "No longer! I am now a man set free!"

For the next five minutes the room shook with the audience's peals of laughter and applause. Everyone pushed their way to that brother, cheering, laughing, and singing. Then they pulled him over to Paul. The two embraced, while over and again the man cried: "Forgive me. Forgive me."

Paul later confessed that the muscles on his face hurt from smiling so long. Titus told me he heard Paul murmur: "At last, something good has come out of Drachrachma!"

Paul eventually managed to get back to answering questions. He finished by telling the story of the last few months, then concluded by telling of his journey to Greece and of the joyful good-bye at Dyrrhachium as some forty brothers and sisters sailed off to Italy to join Priscilla and Aquila in Rome. And last of all, he told of his journey to the little known region of Dalmatia.

"Perhaps Corinth . . . *and* Cenchrea, can take the gospel there," enthused Phoebe, a devout woman from nearby Cenchrea.

Suddenly, all over the room came shouts of "I'll go! I'll go!"

"Good," called out Timothy, "for we eight have decided we also want to proclaim Christ in Dalmatia!"

Paul was astounded, for he knew nothing of this colluding.

Still, the meeting did not end.

The men who were accompanying Paul began to report on what their last three years of being trained had been like. Again and again the room resounded with laughter as each man told hilarious stories about one another. But what was most pleasing to all was the obvious fact that those men were bound together by an unbreakable unity—a unity that matched that of the Twelve.

Everyone there took comfort in knowing that Paul had lived to see such a day. They agreed and said, "Paul walks in the knowledge that after he is dead, those men will take his place in the Gentile world."

Dawn was all that could end that meeting. It proved to be the only meeting that had no guard at the door while Paul was there, as rumors continued that the Daggermen were nearing Corinth. Oddly, this only strengthened the unity of the church in Corinth, as the Corinthian brothers worked hard to make sure there was never a moment Paul was alone.

In the meantime, Paul vacillated somewhere between mild irritation to outright frustration about "such unnecessary overprotection." Nonetheless, he was a brother who virtually always yielded to the will of the church, and this situation was no exception.

A few days later Tertius arrived from Philippi. Paul was openly pleased at having this brother with him again. Soon Paul was having long sessions with Tertius, explaining in detail what he planned to say in his letter to the gathering in Rome.

It now falls to me, Priscilla, to tell you about that remarkable letter. You know, of course, when that letter arrived in Rome, it was first placed in my hands . . . by *Phoebe* of Cenchrea! Before I tell you more, I must give you my very prejudiced opinion. I believe it was, and still is, the greatest piece of literature ever penned by a believer in Christ.

CHAPTER 15

Paul worked for weeks on his letter to those of us in Rome. The letter proved to be somewhat of a condensation of all that Paul considered central to the Christian life.

It is not well known that the letter was built on *messages* delivered in Corinth. Out of spoken messages brought to the church in Corinth emerged the letter he sent to us in Rome.

Every day for a week Paul and Tertius secluded themselves from everyone else. (I am told it took a full day for Paul to dictate and correct just the first three pages.) While in Corinth, Paul stayed in the home of a local brother who had a very large house, large enough to hold meetings to which *everyone* in the Corinthian ecclesia could come. His name was Gaius (not Gaius of Derbe—another Gaius, of Corinth, Greece). Gaius had a servant named Quartus, who was ever at Paul's side and who slept in front of his door.

The Daggermen would have faced a formidable foe had they broken into Gaius's home. Even Timothy and Titus had difficulty seeing Paul, and their curiosity about the letter grew with every passing day. Everyone, except Luke, had a difficult time getting to talk to Paul. Luke stayed in the same house as Paul.

One day Titus and Timothy found Tertius alone, on his way to the home of Gaius.

"What is he saying? What is in that letter?" Titus asked Tertius.

"Remember when Paul spoke to the assembly, presenting a great courtroom drama—with all humanity present, all the people of the world on trial? The throng was divided into two groups. One group—the Gentiles, the other group—the Jews. In the meeting Paul drew us a word picture of how both sides contended they were innocent! Both Jew and Gentile proclaimed that they deserved to be seen as righteous before God. Remember?"

"It was riveting," replied Titus.

"Well, he turned that message into a written drama. It is depicted in the first three pages. Both groups await a verdict. The prosecution uses its own standard to judge each group. Then comes the verdict of the judge."

"What was the verdict?" asked Titus anxiously.

"I know," interrupted Timothy. "You uncircumcised were condemned."

"You are absolutely right!" proclaimed Tertius. "But so were you Jews."

"Aha! I knew it," exclaimed Titus.

"All were found guilty by *their own* standard of what constitutes righteousness. There has never been anything like this letter. I doubt there will be anything like it ever again," continued Tertius in quiet wonder.

"What did he write next?" prodded Timothy.

Tertius shrugged. "I do not know. That is where Paul stopped. Right now, everyone is condemned, with no apparent way out, both the Jews and Gentiles . . . but always, the Jews *first*."

"Oh, my! I hope page four gets better!" muttered a crestfallen Timothy.

"Yes, Timothy . . . you had better hope *very* hard, because right now you are under *double* condemnation," responded Titus. "You are a Jew *and* a Greek!"

"I must go," said Tertius.

Both Titus and Timothy walked with Tertius to the home of Gaius, bombarding Tertius with questions as they walked along.

"Where will Paul be tonight? At Gaius's house?" called Titus.

"No," replied Tertius. "He and I will be at Jason's home this evening."

Timothy and Titus came to Jason's house late that evening, trying again to get any information at all from Tertius.

The entire assembly soon caught this fever. Any word of what Paul was writing soon echoed throughout the gatherings.

One evening Tertius, very excited, sought out Titus and Timothy.

"On pages four and five Paul continues the drama. He presents *another* way to be made righteous. It turns out there is still *one* last hope for both Jews and Gentiles. But only *one*; otherwise, both were condemned."

"Their hope is Jesus Christ!" blurted Titus.

"Obviously!" responded Tertius. "But, oh, the way Paul presented it. He brings in Moses, David, even Adam, to testify that righteousness before God comes only through faith in Jesus Christ."

"What else?"

"That is as far as he has dictated," Tertius said. "Somehow, though, I have the impression that what Paul writes next has to do with . . . well . . . something that tells the Romans, and all of us, the very heart of the walk of believers who are in the church. I could see it in Paul's eyes."

The next evening came and went with no sign of Paul or

Tertius. Sometime after midnight Titus and Timothy gave up and retired for the night.

Paul decided to take a day of rest. (Actually, Paul virtually never rested! He had announced that he would speak to the entire assembly and needed a day to prepare for that meeting.)

The next day Paul announced he wanted to speak to the assembly on the morrow. As a result Tertius had a day to write out a complete and finished copy of pages six, seven, and eight of Paul's letter to those of us in Rome.

All eight of Paul's young men, as well as Luke and Jason, got together and read those three pages to one another.

What they heard left them in awe.

Years later, in Rome, several of those men told me what it was like to read those three pages for the first time. I understand what they mean. Pages six, seven, and eight of that letter seemed to sum up everything we Christians will ever need to understand about living the Christian life.

Please remember that I read that same letter in Rome only a few weeks later. In fact, when the letter arrived in Rome—in the possession of Phoebe—it was into my hands that letter was first placed. I shall never forget what happened to me when *I* read pages six, seven, and eight of that incredible letter.

May I share with you my own experience—the experience I had when reading these pages? That hour was the highlight of my entire life. The letter Paul penned arrived only weeks after he finished it. I have always counted it a sacred privilege that I was the first person in Italy to ever read Paul's letter to those of us in Rome.

Here is the story.

CHAPTER 16

That day in Rome, when Paul's letter arrived, is the most memorable day of my life.

I was standing outside my home on Aventine Hill when I heard the gate open. Some of the young men come from Galatia, who were staying in my house, made a clatter—loud even by their standards—for the gate. Then I heard the word *Phoebe*. Instantly I sprang toward the entrance myself. There stood a beaming Phoebe of Cenchrea!

We ran toward one another and embraced.

Phoebe looked wonderful. How could a woman sail all the way from Corinth, Greece, to Rome, Italy, and arrive at my home relaxed and radiant?

It was not long before my living room was filled with brothers and sisters eager to meet Phoebe and to hear of the assemblies in Greece. We agreed that the assembly in Rome would gather the next night to hear a complete report from Phoebe. I then insisted that Phoebe be allowed to rest.

Then, just as I was showing Phoebe her room, she reached into a leather pouch and handed me four scrolls.

"Do you remember when Aquila, standing on the shores of the Adriatic Sea—just before your ship departed for

Rome—asked Paul to write a letter to the assembly that was being formed in Rome?"

"Yes!" I exclaimed. "Has Paul written such a letter?"

"My dear sister in Christ," said Phoebe, "Paul has not only written that letter, but he has written it magnificently. I am about to hand you what I consider to be one of the most intriguing letters that you will *ever* read."

(I feel that Phoebe was being conservative. In my own opinion the letter Paul wrote to us here in Rome is, without question, the most powerful piece of literature I ever read. And I wonder if it will ever be superseded.)

Phoebe then handed me the four scrolls, which totaled sixteen pages in all.

That night, while sitting all alone beneath a brightly lit torch, I read the entire letter. I wept profusely when I came to the last page. Paul remembered us all—*everyone* he sent to Rome! And what beautiful words of admonition.

I could not help but laugh when I read the part that said: "Greetings to Priscilla and Aquila, who have risked their necks. . . ." It was true! As Roman citizens we could very well have had our heads chopped off by coming back into Rome at a time when my husband, Aquila . . . a Jew . . . had been banished from Rome.

But this is not the story that I wish to tell you.

I wish to tell you what it was that happened to *me* when I read page six. In reading that page, I was hearing it the wrong way! Dear reader, let me share that mistake with you. While reading page six, I took every word Paul said as words written to an individual.

Let me explain. I heard Paul saying to the individual: "Reckon yourself dead." I heard Paul telling *me*, Priscilla, to consider myself as someone who was dead. Perhaps others who read this sixth page will make the same error that I did. And an error it is.

Suddenly something swept over me. It was almost as though I heard the voice of the Lord. And just as quickly I saw what Paul was really saying, and to whom he was saying it. Paul's whole life, Paul's thoughts, *everything* was always on the church. He had written his letter to the *assembly* in Rome, not to an individual! Nor had he written to a group of individuals.

Immediately I realized that it was not for *me* to consider *myself* dead. It was not for a woman named Priscilla to say: "I reckon myself dead." Like lightning striking at my heart and thunder roaring in my head, I realized Paul was writing to a corporate body. He was writing to the ecclesia in Rome. He was telling not an individual, but an entire assembly: "All of you *together* must consider yourselves as one person, and that one person—the church—must consider herself dead!"

I almost came out of my chair. I began to cry. I knew in that very moment that the assembly in Rome would soon gather, and, in a meeting standing before the Lord as one person, we, a corporate people, would reckon ourselves dead before the Lord Jesus. One corporate person . . . dead!

If ever you should read this sixth page, please remember that it was not written to you, an individual. Its message was, and always shall be, to a body of believers . . . to a church. To an assembly. To the ecclesia. It is for her, the Bride, to reckon herself dead to sin.

And, truly, a few days later, we all gathered in one of the parks outside the city wall. There we knelt. And there, we, the ecclesia in Rome, offered ourselves as dead. Yes, it was a *group* of people (perhaps fifty in number). But no, it was not fifty people—it was *one* person. It was the *Bride* of Christ who knelt that day, in a park, and offered herself as being dead to sin and alive to Christ. If you please, the new species in Christ Jesus is completely dead to sin.

When we knelt, we knelt as that Bride. That sixth page

became a reality, not to us as individuals, but as the very body of Christ.

How foolish could I have been! There was hardly a word on that sixth page that was written in single tense. It was all "we" and "us" and "you" plural. It was so obvious that Paul was writing to the entire church. His words were written in the plural, not in the singular. Paul meant for an entire church to be dead to sin and alive to Christ.

Read it here for yourself.

> Well then, should we keep on sinning so that God can show us more and more kindness and forgiveness? Of course not! Since we have died to sin, how can we continue to live in it? Or have you forgotten that when we became Christians and were baptized to become one with Christ Jesus, we died with him? For we died and were buried with Christ by baptism. And just as Christ was raised from the dead by the glorious power of the Father, now we also may live new lives.
>
> Since we have been united with him in his death, we will also be raised as he was. Our old sinful selves were crucified with Christ so that sin might lose its power in our lives. We are no longer slaves to sin. For when we died with Christ we were set free from the power of sin. And since we died with Christ, we know we will also share his new life. We are sure of this because Christ rose from the dead, and he will never die again. Death no longer has any power over him. He died once to defeat sin, and now he lives for the glory of God. So you should consider yourselves dead to sin and able to live for the glory of God through Christ Jesus.
>
> Do not let sin control the way you live; do not give in to its lustful desires. Do not let any part of your body become a tool of wickedness, to be used for sinning. Instead, give yourselves completely to God since you have been given new life. And use your whole body as a tool to do what is right for the

glory of God. Sin is no longer your master, for you are no longer subject to the law, which enslaves you to sin. Instead, you are free by God's grace.

So since God's grace has set us free from the law, does this mean we can go on sinning? Of course not! Don't you realize that whatever you choose to obey becomes your master? You can choose sin, which leads to death, or you can choose to obey God and receive his approval. Thank God! Once you were slaves of sin, but now you have obeyed with all your heart the new teaching God has given you. Now you are free from sin, your old master, and you have become slaves to your new master, righteousness.

I speak this way, using the illustration of slaves and masters, because it is easy to understand. Before, you let yourselves be slaves of impurity and lawlessness. Now you must choose to be slaves of righteousness so that you will become holy.

In those days, when you were slaves of sin, you weren't concerned with doing what was right. And what was the result? It was not good, since now you are ashamed of the things you used to do, things that end in eternal doom. But now you are free from the power of sin and have become slaves of God. Now you do those things that lead to holiness and result in eternal life. For the wages of sin is death, but the free gift of God is eternal life through Christ Jesus our Lord.

But this is not all of my experience. There was still page seven. And page eight! Something just as great happened to me when I read the seventh page. And even more, beyond all words, happened to me when I read that *eighth* page!

CHAPTER 17

You might be surprised if I tell you that I find that seventh page of the letter to us Romans to be my favorite. Here is what happened to me as I read that page.

On page seven, Paul was telling us of his struggle with the law of Moses. Page seven was the biography of Paul, as a Pharisee, a man trying so hard to live up to all those six hundred Jewish rules, regulations, and laws set down by Moses. It all became so beautiful as I realized that the law of Moses had driven Paul of Tarsus to Christ!

But once more a revelation, straight out of my spirit and straight from the Lord, broke in upon me like blinding light. Christians also struggle to "be a good Christian." And they always end up failing. Always!

This page was not only the biography of a Jew trying to live up to the Jewish standards. Paul was saying, "I tried to live a good Jewish life . . . and I kept failing." This could just as well be the biography of a Christian struggling to live a good Christian life—and failing *miserably*.

I paused. I reread the page. My eyes opened wide. I was startled. My trembling fingers traced every line. In every place where Paul said that he was struggling to fulfill the law of

Moses I heard myself saying, "And Christians do the same thing when they try to live the Christian life."

I know! *I* have struggled to live "a good Christian life." I suppose it is our religious nature to try to do these things. Yet there is no Christian life, and there is no living out of the Christian life. There is only Christ.

That is what Paul was saying. Whether you are a Jew without salvation or a Gentile Christian—none of us can live up to our standards of what we ought to be, or what we think God wants.

I read page seven yet again. I read it as one who is a follower of Jesus Christ. This is how I read the passage: "That which I tried to do as a Christian, to please God, I could not do. And the things that I knew a Christian should not do, I went ahead and did them anyway."

Just as Paul, the Jew, cried out: "Oh, what a miserable person I am!" I, Priscilla, cried out: "Oh, what a miserable woman I am! I cannot live the Christian life! Who shall deliver me from the struggles of trying to live the Christian life?"

I abandoned myself to tears as I read what Paul had written next. "Thanks be to God, it is through Jesus Christ!"

Paul struggled to live up to impossible standards, and I, Priscilla, tried so hard to live the Christian life, but we were both failing. And for both of us, there was the same solution: Jesus Christ.

The greatest revelation I have ever had in my life came to me that night: I cannot live the Christian life. I fail! What freedom, what joy, swept over me as I cried: "Lord, only you can live the Christian life."

We Christians cannot live the Christian life. If we try, we *will* fail. We will try so hard to please our Lord—always trying to find something to do that will make God like us more. How foolish! We are already holy and blameless in his eyes. It is only Christ who lives the Christian life.

Please read this seventh page of Paul's letter to Rome as if your name were in it. Let it release you from your struggle to be a perfect Christian, to live the Christian life. Allow this page to speak to you as well:

Now, dear brothers and sisters—you who are familiar with the law—don't you know that the law applies only to a person who is still living? Let me illustrate. When a woman marries, the law binds her to her husband as long as he is alive. But if he dies, the laws of marriage no longer apply to her. So while her husband is alive, she would be committing adultery if she married another man. But if her husband dies, she is free from that law and does not commit adultery when she remarries.

So this is the point: The law no longer holds you in its power, because you died to its power when you died with Christ on the cross. And now you are united with the one who was raised from the dead. As a result, you can produce good fruit, that is, good deeds for God. When we were controlled by our old nature, sinful desires were at work within us, and the law aroused these evil desires that produced sinful deeds, resulting in death. But now we have been released from the law, for we died with Christ, and we are no longer captive to its power. Now we can really serve God, not in the old way by obeying the letter of the law, but in the new way, by the Spirit.

Well then, am I suggesting that the law of God is evil? Of course not! The law is not sinful, but it was the law that showed me my sin. I would never have known that coveting is wrong if the law had not said, "Do not covet." But sin took advantage of this law and aroused all kinds of forbidden desires within me! If there were no law, sin would not have that power.

I felt fine when I did not understand what the law

demanded. But when I learned the truth, I realized I had broken the law and was a sinner, doomed to die. So the good law, which was supposed to show me the way of life, instead gave me the death penalty. Sin took advantage of the law and fooled me; it took the good law and used it to make me guilty of death. But still, the law itself is holy and right and good.

But how can that be? Did the law, which is good, cause my doom? Of course not! Sin used what was good to bring about my condemnation. So we can see how terrible sin really is. It uses God's good commandment for its own evil purposes.

The law is good, then. The trouble is not with the law but with me, because I am sold into slavery, with sin as my master. I don't understand myself at all, for I really want to do what is right, but I don't do it. Instead, I do the very thing I hate. I know perfectly well that what I am doing is wrong, and my bad conscience shows that I agree that the law is good. But I can't help myself, because it is sin inside me that makes me do these evil things.

I know I am rotten through and through so far as my old sinful nature is concerned. No matter which way I turn, I can't make myself do right. I want to, but I can't. When I want to do good, I don't. And when I try not to do wrong, I do it anyway. But if I am doing what I don't want to do, I am not really the one doing it; the sin within me is doing it.

It seems to be a fact of life that when I want to do what is right, I inevitably do what is wrong. I love God's law with all my heart. But there is another law at work within me that is at war with my mind. This law wins the fight and makes me a slave to the sin that is still within me. Oh, what a miserable person I am! Who will free me from this life that is dominated by sin? Thank God! The answer is in Jesus Christ our Lord. So you see how it is: In my mind I really want to obey God's law, but because of my sinful nature I am a slave to sin.

It was almost dawn when I turned over the sheet and came to the eighth page.

I made the same mistake on page eight I had made when I read page six. I began looking at the eighth page as though it were written to an individual. I read that page through. It must be the most beautiful piece of literature ever penned. Page eight is achingly beautiful. Still, I was reading that page in the wrong way!

About halfway through I noticed that virtually every reference was not to a "me," singular. Paul's words were once again in the plural.

Once more I stopped and began to cry.

"Lord, let me see what Paul is writing here. Let me see from his view. And from *your* view. You are not talking to *me*. I know that I am not capable of being a lone, singular, conqueror! Let me see that these glorious words were written for the assembly that gathers here in this city. She is that conqueror. Let me see that every word has to do with a Christian who is living within the assembly.

"I have seen it, Lord! The Christian life and the ecclesia life are inseparable."

So I also reread this page. Every time I saw the plural word *you* I inserted these words in place of the plural *you: the assembly of Jesus Christ that gathers in Rome.*

I was overwhelmed. I could not help but stand and lift my arms to the heavens and thank God that the "you" was plural. In every line of page eight, Paul was speaking to the entire ecclesia. I was but a part of that glorious statement in Romans, page eight!

I cried out: "Lord, deliver me from ever seeing this page as though it were for an individual. Put me in the middle of the community of the believers! Keep me there, centered inside the ecclesia. Always keep my eyes open to forever know that Paul was speaking of all . . . in the assembly! Oh, this triumphant passage has relevance to me only as I live within the practice and experience of the body of Christ.

"Lord, keep me forever in this assembly, that the words of this eighth page might forever be true for me, and not only for me, but for all my brothers and sisters with whom I gather."

So, dear reader, I offer that eighth page to you as I saw it that night. I ask you to remember that you cannot separate the Christian life from the life of the ecclesia. Living within the community of the body of Christ, wherever you are—Ephesus, Corinth, or _____. *That* is the only place the Christian life can be a life lived in victory.

> So now there is no condemnation for those who belong to Christ Jesus. For the power of the life-giving Spirit has freed you through Christ Jesus from the power of sin that leads to death. The law of Moses could not save us, because of our sinful nature. But God put into effect a different plan to save us. He sent his own Son in a human body like ours, except that ours are sinful. God destroyed sin's control over us by giving his Son as a sacrifice for our sins. He did this so that the requirement of the law would be fully accomplished for us who no longer follow our sinful nature but instead follow the Spirit.
>
> Those who are dominated by the sinful nature think about sinful things, but those who are controlled by the Holy Spirit think about things that please the Spirit. If your sinful nature controls your mind, there is death. But if the Holy Spirit controls your mind, there is life and peace. For the sinful nature is always hostile to God. It never did obey God's laws, and it never will. That's why those who are still under the control of their sinful nature can never please God.
>
> But you are not controlled by your sinful nature. You are controlled by the Spirit if you have the Spirit of God living in

you. (And remember that those who do not have the Spirit of Christ living in them are not Christians at all.) Since Christ lives within you, even though your body will die because of sin, your spirit is alive because you have been made right with God. The Spirit of God, who raised Jesus from the dead, lives in you. And just as he raised Christ from the dead, he will give life to your mortal body by this same Spirit living within you.

So, dear brothers and sisters, you have no obligation whatsoever to do what your sinful nature urges you to do. For if you keep on following it, you will perish. But if through the power of the Holy Spirit you turn from it and its evil deeds, you will live. For all who are led by the Spirit of God are children of God.

So you should not be like cowering, fearful slaves. You should behave instead like God's very own children, adopted into his family —calling him "Father, dear Father." For his Holy Spirit speaks to us deep in our hearts and tells us that we are God's children. And since we are his children, we will share his treasures—for everything God gives to his Son, Christ, is ours, too. But if we are to share his glory, we must also share his suffering.

Yet what we suffer now is nothing compared to the glory he will give us later. For all creation is waiting eagerly for that future day when God will reveal who his children really are. Against its will, everything on earth was subjected to God's curse. All creation anticipates the day when it will join God's children in glorious freedom from death and decay. For we know that all creation has been groaning as in the pains of childbirth right up to the present time. And even we Christians, although we have the Holy Spirit within us as a foretaste of future glory, also groan to be released from pain and suffering. We, too, wait anxiously for that day when God will give us our full rights as his children, including the new bodies he has promised us. Now that we are saved, we eagerly look forward to this freedom. For if you already have something, you don't need to hope for it. But if we look forward to something we don't have yet, we must wait patiently and confidently.

And the Holy Spirit helps us in our distress. For we don't even know what we should pray for, nor how we should pray. But the Holy Spirit prays for us with groanings that cannot be expressed in words. And the Father who knows all hearts knows what the Spirit is saying, for the Spirit pleads for us believers in harmony with God's own will. And we know that God causes everything to work together for the good of those who love God and are called according to his purpose for them. For God knew his people in advance, and he chose them to become like his Son, so that his Son would be the firstborn, with many brothers and sisters. And having chosen them, he called them to come to him. And he gave them right standing with himself, and he promised them his glory.

What can we say about such wonderful things as these? If God is for us, who can ever be against us? Since God did not spare even his own Son but gave him up for us all, won't God, who gave us Christ, also give us everything else?

Who dares accuse us whom God has chosen for his own? Will God? No! He is the one who has given us right standing with himself. Who then will condemn us? Will Christ Jesus? No, for he is the one who died for us and was raised to life for us and is sitting at the place of highest honor next to God, pleading for us.

Can anything ever separate us from Christ's love? Does it mean he no longer loves us if we have trouble or calamity, or are persecuted, or are hungry or cold or in danger or threatened with death? (Even the Scriptures say, "For your sake we are killed every day; we are being slaughtered like sheep.") No, despite all these things, overwhelming victory is ours through Christ, who loved us.

And I am convinced that nothing can ever separate us from his love. Death can't, and life can't. The angels can't, and the demons can't. Our fears for today, our worries about tomorrow, and even the powers of hell can't keep God's love away. Whether we are high above the sky or in the deepest ocean, nothing in all creation will ever be able to separate us from the love of God that is revealed in Christ Jesus our Lord.

I have told you of what happened to me when I read the sixth, seventh, and eighth pages of that letter which Paul penned in Corinth and sent to Rome.

I am told that Timothy, Titus, Jason, and all the other brothers were just as stunned when they read those same pages handed to them by Tertius.

So let us return to Corinth.

I would remind you that Paul had taken a day to rest in order to prepare a message he wanted to bring to the assembly in Corinth.

So return with me to the place where the letter to the Romans was written. Return with me to Corinth, to Jason's home, to those who first read pages six, seven, and eight. And to the meeting of the entire church in Corinth, where Paul delivered a most unique message. What Paul had to say to the Corinthians was remarkable.

C H A P T E R   1 8

Tonight I desire to speak to you about problems. *Church* problems. Problems we all face being so close to one another. That is, problems we have in being in the body of Christ. The conflicts that come out of our knowing one another *too well.* In fact, I am going to touch on just about *every* major problem I have ever witnessed in any . . . and all . . . the Gentile churches. *All* of them. Obviously, life together does pose its crises!"

The room rocked with the assembly's laughter.

"It will be a long night!" Secundus chuckled.

"Very long," added Jason.

"I have a list," added Paul, holding up a piece of paper. "When I have gone through this list of problems we so frequently run across in the church, I will include the entire list in the letter I am writing to the believers gathered in Rome. I do this in hopes that the Roman believers will learn from all of our experiences of living together. At least they will know the litany of problems that come out of life together in the ecclesia."

Paul began his message that night by reminding everyone of the mercies of God toward them. And yes, his message that night was quite similar to several of the pages of the letter he wrote to us in Rome.

And so, dear brothers and sisters, I plead with you to give your bodies to God. Let them be a living and holy sacrifice—the kind he will accept. When you think of what he has done for you, is this too much to ask? Don't copy the behavior and customs of this world, but let God transform you into a new person by changing the way you think. Then you will know what God wants you to do, and you will know how good and pleasing and perfect his will really is.

After those opening words, Paul wrote four pages covering problems that are frequently found in life in the community of the church. In doing so, he rendered a great service to the church in Rome. We in Rome eventually passed through virtually every crisis Paul covered in those four pages. But not just us. What he said applies to all the assemblies. All the churches have these problems. And why not? When God's people are involved in one another's lives every waking moment, problems come out! And those problems are predictable. What Paul said to those of us in the life of one church fits all who are together in ecclesia life.

You might wish to read those four pages. This is what all believers face as we live together.

So I pray that God, who gives you hope, will keep you happy and full of peace as you believe in him. May you overflow with hope through the power of the Holy Spirit.

I am fully convinced, dear brothers and sisters, that you are full of goodness. You know these things so well that you are able to teach others all about them. Even so, I have been bold enough to emphasize some of these points, knowing that all you need is this reminder from me. For I am, by God's grace, a special messenger from Christ Jesus to you Gentiles. I bring you the Good News and offer you up as a fragrant sacrifice to God so that you might be pure and pleasing to him by the Holy Spirit. So it is right for me to be enthusiastic about all Christ Jesus has done through me in my service to God. I dare not boast of anything else. I have brought the Gentiles to God by my message and by the way I lived before them. I have won them over by the miracles done through me as signs from God—all by the power of God's Spirit. In this way, I have fully presented the Good News of Christ all the way from Jerusalem clear over into Illyricum.

My ambition has always been to preach the Good News where the name of Christ has never been heard, rather than where a church has already been started by someone else. I have been following the plan spoken of in the Scriptures, where it says, "Those who have never been told about him will see, and those who have never heard of him will understand."

Paul finished that page by telling the Roman church of his plans to come to Rome as soon as possible. He now needed only to finish the letter. He took a full page to do so. Paul gave greetings by mentioning the names of those of us in Rome . . . that is, those whose names he could remember. (Alas, he forgot *several* people's names.)

Then came Paul's last words.

Timothy, Luke, Sopater (Sopater was called Sosipater while he was in Rome, as that is the Latin form of his name), Jason, Paul's host Gaius, as well as Erasmus, the city treasurer—these men were all in the room with Paul at the time he finished the letter. He also mentioned Quartus, Paul's guard.

Here was a very intimate close, written in Paul's own hand. If ever you should happen to read that close, imagine what it was like for about forty-five believers gathered in my home in Rome as they first read this warm benediction!

Greet Priscilla and Aquila. They have been co-workers in my ministry for Christ Jesus. In fact, they risked their lives for me. I am not the only one who is thankful to them; so are all the Gentile churches. Please give my greetings to the church that meets in their home.

Greet my dear friend Epenetus. He was the very first person to become a Christian in the province of Asia. Give my greetings to Mary, who has worked so hard for your benefit. Then there are Andronicus and Junia, my relatives, who were in prison with me. They are respected among the apostles and became Christians before I did. Please give them my greetings. Say hello to Ampliatus, whom I love as one of the Lord's own children, and Urbanus, our co-worker in Christ, and beloved Stachys.

Give my greetings to Apelles, a good man whom Christ approves. And give my best regards to the members of the household of Aristobulus. Greet Herodion, my relative. Greet the Christians in the household of Narcissus. Say hello to Tryphena and Tryphosa, the Lord's workers, and to dear Persis, who has worked so hard for the Lord. Greet Rufus, whom the Lord picked out to be his very own; and also his dear mother, who has been a mother to me.

And please give my greetings to Asyncritus, Phlegon, Hermes, Patrobas, Hermas, and the brothers and sisters who are with them. Give my greetings to Philologus, Julia, Nereus and his sister, and to Olympas and all the other believers who are with them. Greet each other in Christian love. All the churches of Christ send you their greetings.

And now I make one more appeal, my dear brothers and sisters. Watch out for people who cause divisions and upset people's faith by teaching things that are contrary to what you have been taught. Stay away from them. Such people are not serving Christ our Lord; they are serving their own personal interests. By smooth talk and glowing words they deceive innocent people. But everyone knows that you are obedient to the Lord. This makes me very happy. I want you to see clearly what is right and to stay innocent of any wrong. The God of peace will soon crush Satan under your feet. May the grace of our Lord Jesus Christ be with you.

Timothy, my fellow worker, and Lucius, Jason, and Sosipater, my relatives, send you their good wishes.

I, Tertius, the one who is writing this letter for Paul, send my greetings, too, as a Christian brother.

Gaius says hello to you. I am his guest, and the church meets here in his home. Erastus, the city treasurer, sends you his greetings, and so does Quartus, a Christian brother.

God is able to make you strong, just as the Good News says. It is the message about Jesus Christ and his plan for you Gentiles, a plan kept secret from the beginning of time. But now as the prophets foretold and as the eternal God has commanded, this message is made known to all Gentiles everywhere, so that they might believe and obey Christ. To God, who alone is wise, be the glory forever through Jesus Christ. Amen.

Now only one thing was lacking. How to get the letter safely to Rome? This was no small problem. Neither was the solution.

CHAPTER 19

I have heard it said that Paul chose Phoebe to deliver the Roman letter because she was planning a business trip to Rome anyway. Not so—Paul chose Phoebe because of his great confidence in her. Paul *sent* Phoebe from Greece to join us in Rome.

Phoebe is, as I am, a Roman citizen, not to mention that she is also a shrewd businesswoman. (Not long after she came to Rome she set up a business that allowed several brothers and sisters to find work.) But Paul chose Phoebe primarily because of her love for Christ.

Now I will tell you a little-known story.

Shortly before Phoebe departed, Paul decided to add three more pages to his letter. The three pages were mostly about the Jews' relationship to Jesus Christ. Just as Phoebe boarded the ship Paul thrust the new scroll into her hands.

Paul told her, "Phoebe, you have thirteen pages in the letter you are taking with you to Rome. Here are three more pages. Please find some place within the letter where you can place these three pages. I suggest you place them immediately after page three . . . or after page eight."

Phoebe chose to insert these additional three pages just after page *eight*. (I, Priscilla, always felt those pages would have fit in much more clearly had they been inserted after page *three!*)

There on the ship Tertius made one more addition to the letter. At the *top* of the *last* page he squeezed in these words:

> Our sister Phoebe, a deacon in the church in Cenchrea, will be coming to see you soon. Receive her in the Lord, as one who is worthy of high honor. Help her in every way you can, for she has helped many in their needs, including me.

As the ship pulled out, brothers and sisters from the churches in Corinth and Cenchrea stood on the docks and waved good-bye to their beloved Phoebe.

It was at this time that the Daggermen arrived in Corinth, their daggers, and their prayers, dedicated to Paul.

I must tell you that story. First, though, you may be asking: "When Aquila arrived in Italy, was he, a Jew, allowed into Rome? Was he beheaded for entering the city, thereby breaking the decree of Claudius—the decree that stated that *all* Jews stay out of Rome on penalty of death?"

CHAPTER 20

When Aquila and I and those five single brothers from Galatia arrived at the gates of Rome, Aquila did not enter but stayed in the countryside just outside the city.

I went straight to our new house on Aventine Hill. For several days I inquired of every friend and acquaintance I had in the city (and there were many, including those in Caesar's houshold), "Are there any Jews who have dared to return to Rome? What is Nero's attitude toward Claudius's decree and toward the Jews?"

"Forget Nero," I was told. "Nero is a child. *Seneca* rules the empire. His attitude toward the Jews is nonexistent. No one knows the answer to your question."

Some Jews *had* returned to the Trastavere District, and none had been arrested.

I was still unsure of what to do when Aquila resolved the dilemma. The third day after our arrival, he left the countryside and walked into Rome and into our house!

"Here is my neck. Does anyone want it?" he declared as he entered the room.

I laughed with joy as I hugged my beloved husband. I scolded him lightly even though I knew by then that his presence would be tolerated in Rome.

Just after Phoebe arrived, a Roman soldier came to my house. His presence had something to do with my having bought our home as a Roman citizen. For some reason he insisted on seeing proof of my Roman citizenship.

"You do not look like a Roman," he said in the typical threatening manner of Roman soldiers.

"And why is that?" I asked as I walked right up to him, peering into his face.

"You have blue eyes."

Phoebe, speaking more boldly than I had, interrupted: "I have *green* eyes and I am a Roman citizen. Further, you would be wise to discover that Nero also has blue eyes."

"He does?!" replied the startled soldier.

"So did Julius Caesar," Phoebe continued.

"Unbelievable," replied the almost panicked soldier.

I interjected, "Please call me Lady Priscilla."

The man backed away and stammered, "You're acquainted with Caesar's household?"

"I belong to a greater house—that of the King of kings."

The soldier flushed, not sure of what he was hearing.

"Now give me your name so I might report you to the head of the imperial guard for harrassing me," I continued, looking at him expectantly.

The soldier turned ashen and began a hasty retreat for the door. After he left, I hugged Phoebe, and we offered prayers of praise to our God and Savior for preserving our safety.

About six months later, Jews did begin to return to Rome in small numbers. The first were the leaders of the Jewish synagogue. Then came others. A few were believers. It is because of Paul's foresight that those believing Jews *had* to become part of a *Gentile* assembly. And that is as it should be, for Rome *is* a Gentile city.

(The church in Rome was virtually annihilated seven years later. But even today, a generation after that calamity, the church in Rome is Gentile to the core, still reflecting the city's ethos.)

Now let us return to Corinth . . . and the Daggermen.

They have arrived, Paul. They are in Corinth."

It was Jason. He continued, "They visited the synagogue leaders last evening."

Paul did not need to ask *who* had arrived.

"The wonder is that the Daggermen have taken so long to find me," responded Paul resolutely.

"You must go into hiding, now . . . until we can get you out of the city. Erasmus, the city treasurer, has provided a place for you, with city guards to protect you. Even the *sicarii* will not attack a city official, nor his guards. Quartus will, of course, continue to be with you at all times."

"True, they may not attack Erasmus *unless* they have placed themselves under a *curse*. Even more—a curse with a *deadline!* Then they will attack *anyone* in order to get to me," observed Paul.

Was Paul inwardly disturbed? That answer we will never know. But this is certain: according to all reports, he did not *look* fearful.

"I will have one final meeting with the church," Paul added.

Jason's eyebrows rose. He then turned to one of his servants and whispered something. A few minutes later *nine* men—headed by Luke—were in the room *assuring* Paul that he would not have a last gathering with the church.

"You will stay in hiding until we get you out of here—probably by ship," stated Luke in a voice that did not at all typify the beloved physician.

"I yield," said Paul, "but it will do no good to be secretive. They will find out. And they will find me. We might as well do this in the open. Try to arrange for us to sail from Cenchrea to Troas . . . if at all possible."

"All the ships sailing south are filled with Jews on their way to Jerusalem for the Passover. We have heard that the Daggermen plan to wait until you board ship. The deed is to be done at night," said Jason.

"An excellent plot indeed," sighed Paul, rather fatalistically. "My body dumped into the Adriatic Sea during the night. Clever enough."

"I know a way to foil this plot," said Secundus. (And no one doubted his words, as Secundus had a flare for the creative.)

"Say on," urged Gaius.

"We will board the ship to Troas. Paul will take a ship north, back to Philippi. He will then sail from *Philippi* to Troas."

Secundus continued to embellish his idea. In a few minutes he had everyone laughing and agreeing.

"Now *there* is a counterplot if ever I heard of one," said Paul, slapping his knee.

Paul did meet with the church. It was part of Secundus's plan. Messengers were sent out at the last minute, telling of the place of meeting. Erasmus provided soldiers, with swords, near the meeting room.

Paul spoke for several hours and then, with great emotion, bid everyone good-bye. As the meeting ended, it was openly announced that Paul would be leaving by ship the very next day, en route to Troas.

As planned, early the next morning a company of believers made their way to the seaport town of Cenchrea. There they dutifully awaited the hoisting of sails by the ship on which they had bought passage.

One of the men boarding the ship was closely surrounded by Tychicus, Trophimus, Timothy, Titus, Aristarchus, and Sopater. This mysterious man was low of stature, his head was covered, and he walked with a stride that matched Paul's perfectly. Further, this man was treated with great respect by all who were with him, nor did they ever cease looking around for possible danger. The cloaked figure was, of course, Secundus, playing his role of imitating Paul's eccentricities to perfection. That day ended all doubt: Secundus was a born actor.

It did not go unnoticed that a company of Jews wearing the garb of rural Judea also boarded the same ship, their faces stern and cold.

In the meantime, Paul and Luke slipped out of the city, and instead of going north to Philippi by ship, the two men *walked* to Philippi.

That night Secundus, while hiding behind some deck cargo, removed his cloak and threw the garment overboard. The next morning the ever-somber *sicarii* found themselves facing a boisterous, uproarious, group of young men going out of their way to enjoy themselves.

For several days the *sicarii* went from one end of the ship to the other trying to find the little man, but he was . . . well . . . nowhere to be found. The day before reaching Troas, one of the Daggermen, in anger and frustration, approached the brothers and asked where Paul was.

"Paul?" echoed Secundus. "Paul who?"

The rest of the young men barely managed to keep straight faces.

The irrepressible Secundus was to have one last moment of glory. When the ship docked at Troas, Secundus let the

Daggermen disembark first. He then strode down the gang-plank mimicking Paul's walk.

The Daggermen were outraged.

The Eight became very busy once they arrived in Troas. (Not to mention having given a wild, warm, good-bye to the *sicarii* when they sailed on to Jerusalem.) Once the *sicarii* had departed, the eight brothers spread out across the city telling people that Paul of Tarsus would soon be there to proclaim the gospel of Jesus Christ.

Not many days after that, the Philippians awoke one morning to find an unexpected visitor. Paul! On April 27, twenty-eight years after the Lord's resurrection, Paul and Luke celebrated the Feast of Unleavened Bread with their brothers and sisters in Philippi.

Immediately after the Passover, Luke and Paul departed Philippi, taking ship for Troas. The voyage went well, lasting only five days.

Paul remained in Troas a full seven days—something he had never before managed to do.

It is probable that Paul was more welcome in Troas than in any other city on earth. The announcement of his presence was received with great joy by both Jew and Gentile residents. Despite everything that Blastinius Drachrachma had attempted to do in Troas, the synagogue leaders always held Paul in high esteem and welcomed him into their midst.

As expected, Paul's days in Troas were momentous. This city, which Paul had unavoidably had to neglect so many times, responded to every word he spoke. A strong assembly was born in Troas.

"Not since the day we entered Ephesus have I seen such a wonderful beginning," observed Timothy.

To say the least, Paul's company lived in a state of daily joy.

But then, on the last day, tragedy struck.

CHAPTER 22

One of the largest houses in Troas was the place where Paul was speaking, and *it* was not large enough to contain the crowd. After speaking for two hours, Paul dismissed those in the home so that he could speak to the people waiting outside.

It is stuffy in here, thought Luke. *Between the crowd and the lamps, the air is being eaten up in here.*

To get a good seat, one young man, Eutychus by name, climbed up onto a high window. Eutychus eventually fell asleep and tumbled out into the courtyard below. Those who reached him first found a lifeless body.

Luke, one of the first to reach Eutychus, murmured, "This does not look good!"

At that moment Paul arrived. He proceeded to do what Elijah had once done. He stretched his body over the young man, pulled the arms of Eutychus around him, and prayed. Paul then stepped back: "He is alive."

Eutychus began to gasp for air. Paul motioned to Luke and called for some brothers to lift Eutychus. Paul then walked back into the house, there to continue speaking until dawn. He had made every minute in Troas count for his Lord.

There, too, brothers implored Paul *not* to continue on to Jerusalem. The city, everyone knew, was on the verge of a rebellion. The coming festival just might ignite that rebellion.

"Revolt is inevitable," he heard again and again. "Do not be in Jerusalem when it comes."

"Paul, everything we hear tells us you are not welcome in Jerusalem," pleaded the eight young men. "And do not forget the *sicarii!* They are committed to rebellion, with death to anyone and everyone who stands in the way. Every day they select someone allied with Rome, or someone who is perverting the teachings of Moses; . . . they pray for him and kill him."

Paul was adamant. "Only God can turn me from this journey, and I have not heard him speak such words."

Together they walked to the docks of Troas, there to board a waiting ship filled with Jewish pilgrims bound for Jerusalem.

"So many Jews . . . and perhaps assassins." Anxiety over Paul's safety grew. Even Secundus could not come up with a solution to the dilemma.

"I would cherish a few days all alone," said Paul finally. "All of you board the ship. It is not far to the city of Assos, which is the ship's first port of call. It is only twenty-five miles. Right now I need solitude. I will walk. Wait for me in Assos."

And so it was agreed.

A day later, as Paul neared Assos, his thoughts went back to the cities of Magnesia, Pergamum, Philadelphia, Sardis, and other towns where assemblies had been planted by the young men he had sent out from Ephesus. His thoughts then turned to Epaphras, and the assembly in Colosse.

These churches, scattered throughout Asia Minor, must not find themselves cast out of fellowship with the Jewish churches.

Just then he caught sight of a giant block of granite. On the top of this granite hill a heathen temple had been built. *Ah*, he thought, *beyond this rock, Assos.*

By the time Paul entered Assos his heart was set. He was willing to go to his death, but he must see Jerusalem.

Why such commitment?

Paul was engaged in a desperate effort to keep the Gentile and Jewish churches in unity. For him, life was not as important as oneness among the churches.

Having entered Assos, Paul found his companions. Together they found a ship about to sail south. Unfortunately, it was docking at virtually every port in Asia Minor *except* Ephesus. It would dock at Miletus, not far from Ephesus. Paul was running out of time if he still hoped to reach Jerusalem by Pentecost. Still, he wanted to visit Ephesus.

They boarded the ship, sailed past the island of Mitylene and then docked on the island of Samos.

"I have an idea, Luke. It may work," said Paul, just as the ship neared the port of Miletus. "You are a horseman, perhaps you can advise me. How long would it take a swift rider to travel from Miletus to Ephesus?"

So began a plan to arrange for Ephesus to come to Paul!

All cargo that had been taken on board along the way was now unloaded on the wharves of Miletus. The estimated time for the ship to be in Miletus was seven days. Following Luke's plan, Paul sent a message, on horseback, to Ephesus.

"Could the assembly in Ephesus send their elders to Paul in a day's time?"

Only forty hours after the messenger's departure, the Ephesian elders had arrived in Miletus. It was an incredible feat.

Paul had always known the dangers of bestowing the title of elder on any man. He was determined to address the Ephesian elders concerning this danger.

Paul sat down with the elders on the beautiful sandy beach of Miletus. Their first words were admonitions urging him not to go to Jerusalem. This was their report: "She is part of a nation about to attempt to cast off the Roman Empire. The Zealots and *sicarii* grow in number daily. Other secret sects, just as dangerous, have sprung up just in the last few months. And you, Paul, are on everyone's list."

Once more, to his dismay, Paul heard the name Blastinius.

It seems that when Blastinius departed Corinth, he went straight back to Jerusalem. There he raised up an entire group of people whose purpose, like his own, was to destroy Paul's work among the Gentiles.

As to Jerusalem, Paul could not be dissuaded.

None of this was Paul's central intent in this meeting. His burden was to make sure elders *never* ruled over God's people.

(You will note that Paul had written six of his nine letters to churches. Not once in all those six letters did he ever mention elders. He always wrote to *all* the saints!)

As you know, Luke was present in the gathering that day. I can do no better than to record here Luke's own account of what Paul said to the Ephesian elders. (Essentially what Paul said was, "Treat God's people as gently as I have. And remember, *I*, the one who planted this church, have authority, you do not." It was a good word for any elders to hear, but even more important for eight young men who would become church planters to hear.)

"You know that from the day I set foot in the province of Asia until now I have done the Lord's work humbly—yes, and with tears. I have endured the trials that came to me from the plots of the Jews. Yet I never shrank from telling you the truth, either publicly or in your homes. I have had one message for Jews and Gentiles alike—the necessity of turning from sin and turning to God, and of faith in our Lord Jesus.

"And now I am going to Jerusalem, drawn there irresistibly by the Holy Spirit, not knowing what awaits me, except that the Holy Spirit has told me in city after city that jail and suffering lie ahead. But my life is worth nothing unless I use it for doing the work assigned me by the Lord Jesus—the work of telling others the Good News about God's wonderful kindness and love.

"And now I know that none of you to whom I have preached the Kingdom will ever see me again. Let me say plainly that I have been faithful. No one's damnation can be blamed on me, for I didn't shrink from declaring all that God wants for you.

"And now beware! Be sure that you feed and shepherd God's flock—his church, purchased with his blood—over whom the Holy Spirit has appointed you as elders. I know full well that false teachers, like vicious wolves, will come in among you after I leave, not sparing the flock. Even some of you will distort the truth in order to draw a following. Watch out! Remember the three years I was with you—my constant watch and care over you night and day, and my many tears for you.

"And now I entrust you to God and the word of his grace—his message that is able to build you up and give you an inheritance with all those he has set apart for himself.

"I have never coveted anyone's money or fine clothing. You know that these hands of mine have worked to pay my own way, and I have even supplied the needs of those who were with me. And I have been a constant example of how you can help the poor by working hard. You should remember the words of the Lord Jesus: 'It is more blessed to give than to receive.'"

When Paul finished, everyone—Luke, the elders, the Eight, closed in around him and, kneeling, joined together in the most fervent of prayers.

Immediately thereafter, Paul and his company boarded their ship. Just as quickly the ship departed. The elders turned homeward, grim and sobered. It was May 14, exactly twenty-eight years after the Lord's resurrection.

It breaks my heart to add this terrible truth: Most of those Ephesian elders were faithful—for a while—in being ordinary brothers who, on occasion, were called on to lead the church out of a crisis. But as years passed, these men frequently asserted themselves over the other brothers and sisters. Functioning of the body declined. As so often happens, as the years rolled on, some of these men moved closer and closer to becoming dictators. Years later, unfortunately, Paul had to send Timothy to Ephesus to depose these men from their hierarchical conduct. Timothy removed them as elders! (I thank God that there are itinerant church planters with us . . . broken men, humble men, who can prevent local brothers from seizing control of the very body of Christ. May it ever be so! And may every man forever remember the danger of being given a religious title.)

The second day out the ship passed the island of Rhodes. At that very moment, Silas was raising up the church of the Lord Jesus Christ on that island.

Passing Rhodes, the ship came to its intended destination, Patara. By the mercies of God, there at Patara the men found a ship about to sail for Phoenicia. They hardly had time to board before the ship departed. A day later they caught sight of the outline of the island of Cyprus. As they sailed past Cyprus, Paul recounted his first visit to that isle. As Paul told the story Luke took notes as had become his custom.

"We are not far from Antioch," declared Titus, "but we will not be docking there. This ship has its sails set for Tyre, a city that falls within the borders of Syria."

As soon as the ship docked in Tyre, Paul sent Titus into the city to let the ecclesia know of his arrival. The believers in Tyre suddenly found themselves hosting ten unexpected, yet joyously received, guests.

Because the ship required an entire week to unload its cargo, Paul found himself ministering to a large and grateful host of believers. But even in Tyre, Paul heard the same refrain: "We ask you, by the Holy Spirit, do not set foot in Jerusalem."

And his answer was always the same: "I must!"

On the last day of their stopover in Tyre, all the local brothers and sisters and their children passed out of the city onto the beaches. Together they knelt and together they prayed. Having said their good-byes, Paul and his friends boarded yet another ship, one with sails set for the land of Israel.

Some twenty miles south of Tyre the ship approached Ptolemais, the first city actually located inside the borders of Israel. For seven of those men it was the first time their feet trod upon the land God promised Abraham. To say the least, excitement was running high. That night the ten sojourners once more had the privilege of being guests of the ecclesia that gathered in Ptolemais.

It was now just fourteen days before Pentecost.

Departing Ptolemais at dawn, Paul and his companions would walk the rest of the way to Caesarea-by-the-Sea, a city that is *Rome*'s capital of Israel. (But for all Jews, Jerusalem was and always will be *the* capital of Israel.)

How can I communicate to you the high drama that ensued during the next three weeks. Most men could live a thousand years and *never* experience what Paul suffered through those next few days. Those days were seared in the minds of the Eight, beginning with the experience of meeting a Hebrew prophet!

It all had its beginning just as Paul entered Caesarea.

CHAPTER 23

With the shadow of death falling across his face, Paul went straight to the home of Philip the Evangelist. All ten men were warmly welcomed into Philip's home.

That evening Philip held the young workers spellbound while he told them stories of the earliest days of the church. (Yes, and once again Luke took notes.) Philip's last story was about the conversion of an Ethiopian eunuch. Even Paul had never heard that story.

Luke managed to obtain a copy of Mark's story of the life of Jesus. For long hours he did nothing but read, ask questions, and make more notes. Luke was set on fire by the thought of a Gentile's view of the Lord's life. He was soon everywhere, interviewing anyone who had met Jesus or who had been present at Pentecost.

Later, when Luke procured a copy of Matthew's story of the Lord's life, he was heard to mutter: "Why start off a book with a two-page *genealogy?*"

Paul was horrified when he learned that Luke had sent a request to Jerusalem asking to speak with Mary.

"Gall! That took gall," muttered Paul.

Truthfully, Luke did little for the next two years but interview people who knew the Lord intimately and those who were present at Pentecost. Luke once told me he felt he had been given the greatest of all possible gifts when Mark gave him a copy of Barnabas's notes, taken while Barnabas was sitting in Solomon's Colonnade listening to the Twelve and writing down everything they spoke.

The next evening the assembly in Caesarea gathered to hear Paul and to meet his companions. Alas, they were as eager to meet "the Eight" as they were to hear Paul. Already Paul's young men were being called *the Eight* in the same way the original disciples were called *the Twelve*, only this time with a sprinkling of humor added. I was once told, "Paul has raised up eight Gentile church planters, but please remember that one-and-a-half of them are Jews," referring to the fact that Sopater was a Hebrew and Timothy was half-Jewish. Most comments about the Eight were centered on how rowdy they were. True, the Twelve had their humor, but they were also Jewish. The Eight, you must remember, were *heathen*.

The Lord's people in Caesarea had already met Timothy, and some were previously acquainted with Titus, as he had been present at the Jerusalem council some years ago. But the others were totally unknown. Therefore, when they each brought a brief message to the gathering in Caesarea, the Lord's people were, to say the least, curious.

That particular night it was Gaius, rather than Timothy, who won the hour with his furiousity and boldness.

One brother in the Caesarea assembly paid the young men the ultimate compliment: "You men can proclaim the gospel almost as well as Philip's daughters!" (Philip had four daughters, all of whom were extraordinary speakers.)

The next day *Agabus* arrived!

Agabus had come from Jerusalem for the sole purpose of confronting Paul. When he arrived in Caesarea, he went straight to Philip's house. Unannounced, this fierce man who had a flair for the dramatic walked straight up to Paul. Only on rare occasions, always in times of crisis, Agabus had predicted the future. This proved to be one of those times.

Agabus was a stocky man of medium height, with a large, rugged, weather-beaten face, high forehead, and fiery eyes deep-set beneath a heavy brow, which, all combined, made an imposing figure as he stepped in front of Paul. It was Tychicus who whispered everyone's thought: "He looks like one of those prophets of old."

Agabus knelt, took Paul's girdle, and bound it around himself. Then he reached down and tied his own feet and hands.

Ten men stood transfixed at a scene that looked like it had been taken right out of the life of Elijah. Stone-faced, and staring intently at Paul, Agabus pronounced, in a deep rumbling voice:

> "The Holy Spirit declares, 'So shall the owner of this belt be bound by the Jewish leaders in Jerusalem and turned over to the Romans.'"

Without another word, Agabus then turned and left the room. Silence thundered. Then sobs. Several clasped their hands over their mouths, others clamped their fists to their jaws. Luke broke the heavy silence: "Paul, you *must not go!*"

"Paul, this is a word from the Lord," struggled Trophimus.

In a moment, all of the brothers had surrounded Paul, adding their own desperate pleadings.

"He did not say I would die," answered Paul calmly.

"That is not correct," said Gaius. "Agabus did not say the Jews would kill you, but it seems to me he was saying that the Gentiles would."

"Just as it was with Jesus!" breathed Sopater.

Then Philip spoke: "Paul, if such a word were delivered to me, I would assume that if *I* went to Jerusalem *I* would die."

Paul sighed.

"I will ponder this. We still have a few days before the festival of Pentecost begins. I am loath to miss that festival. After all, am I not a good Jew? Is it not my right to go into Jerusalem? It is as much my city as any man's. Timothy, tomorrow you will escort your fellow workers to Jerusalem. I will either be with you . . . or . . . I will remain in Caesarea. I will decide tomorrow."

This man had been shipwrecked, jailed, stoned, whipped, beaten with rods, and yet his most terrifying days lay right before him. These would be days we would all remember as pure horror.

That next morning Paul found himself facing another entrenched group of brothers and sisters. This time it was the church which gathered in Caesarea.

"The same Daggermen who went to Corinth intending to kill you—even now these men are in Jerusalem waiting for you. There are also rumors about Blastinius Drachrachma that are just as foreboding. We beg you—do not go."

Paul's words were slow, but spoken evenly and without emotion.

"The oneness of the churches is at the brink. Preventing that rift is the only thing on earth that is important to me. Years ago, we settled this same issue in Jerusalem. There is only one body—it is Christ's. In each city, only one church. If you are a Jew, you are *there*, in that assembly. If you are a Gentile, you are also *there* in that *one* church in each city. Not being in that one assembly, not even speaking to one another just because of a small piece of skin *cannot* be central! The idea of breaking that oneness is intolerable. Abraham was justified *before* that skin was removed. How dare we enter a city and see *two* gatherings—one Jewish, one Gentile. The angels would weep forever!

"There will be future crises; therefore, we must somehow raise a standard *now*. A standard that declares: Such matters will *not* divide us. A standard of that quality must come out of *Jerusalem*, and Jerusalem alone. My life will be a small price to pay for the raising of that standard."

Paul had turned his face like flint, to Jerusalem and to death . . . and all in the room that day knew it. All, therefore, relinquished. "The Lord's will be done" was the final word.

(Just before Paul's company started out for the Holy City, a man named Mnason joined their group. Mnason, a believer dating back to the earliest days, owned a home in Jerusalem, and for that reason invited everyone in Paul's party to take their lodging in his Jerusalem home.)

The journey to Jerusalem was not at all like the one Timothy had made with Paul some three years earlier. That journey had been accompanied by laughter, stories, and lightheartedness. On *this* journey hardly a word was spoken.

Nevertheless, Paul eventually did begin telling his young friends the history of Jerusalem, going back to David and the Jebusites; yet he centered mostly on that remarkable day when Pentecost was fulfilled . . . an event which had taken place exactly twenty-eight years earlier.

"It was the day of the coming of the Holy Spirit. But also, this ancient festival foretold the birth of the ecclesia. At dawn each year on the morning of Pentecost there are *two* loaves that are cooked in an oven. The mystery of that second loaf was hidden until your lifetime. That first loaf represents the Jewish ecclesia. When Cornelius and those who were gathered with him in his home received the Holy Spirit, we came to understand the meaning of that second loaf. This represented the Gentile assemblies."

Later, on about the third day of their journey, Timothy and Sopater began explaining to the others the tradition of singing the Songs of Ascent upon nearing Jerusalem. So it came about that as they drew near the gates of Jerusalem this small company outsang and outshouted all the other nearby pilgrims.

About a mile out from the city, they noticed a group of men standing by the road who were obviously waiting . . . for someone.

"I know those men," said Timothy.

"I do too," said Titus. "They are some of the leading brothers of the Jerusalem ecclesia."

"Dare we take this as a good omen?" asked Secundus.

"Yes," replied Paul, who immediately left the road, approaching them with outstretched arms.

"Come, Paul," said one. "We will take a not-so-well-traveled route into the city. In a few minutes, outside the view of anyone, we will ask you to put on this robe and this hood. You may not live to make it into the city otherwise. There are spies everywhere seeking to find you."

Paul did not protest. Rather, he asked: "Shall Luke and these young men come with me?"

The Jerusalem brothers conferred for a few moments.

"Choose one who has never been in the city before and is not recognized. The others should go by the traditional route."

Paul turned: "Sopater, you and Timothy lead the brothers to Jerusalem. Gaius, come with me."

Sopater began a mild protest: "I know as little about Jerusalem as Gaius. Maybe less. I never professed to be a *Jewish* Jew."

Gaius's only response was a broad smile and a vigorous wave of good-bye.

Paul soon found himself being led to the home of Mary, the sister of Barnabas. Not long afterward the rest of his company arrived there and an extraordinary meeting followed. Paul and his friends sat down with the elders of the church. James, the brother of Jesus, was even present.

"Brother Paul, by now you must know the situation in this city. The Daggermen are here, and they have but one purpose for their presence: to do away with *you*. Blastinius Drachrachma has stirred up yet others against you. Their hatred of you is at fever pitch. In turn, a new sect, who are now calling themselves the *Zealots*, are plotting to harm you. Beyond that, it seems that almost every man in this city who can read has read a copy of your letter to the Galatians. The city is on the verge of a riot. Fanatics want more than a riot. There are many who are trying to ignite a rebellion. They want a firestorm. There is even an Egyptian here who is doing his best to foment a revolt."

Paul groaned.

"Among those who cannot read, your enemies have made sure they have had the *entire* letter read to them."

"I did not know," replied Paul, obviously shaken, "nor could I have *ever* imagined that when I wrote the letter to the four churches in Galatia, I would be signing my death warrant."

"That may be exactly what you have done," replied one of the elders grimly. "After all, that letter *does* sound like you have denied the teachings of Moses."

The room was silent. Everyone was waiting to see if Paul would give a defense. He said nothing.

"Are you suggesting Paul turn around and leave the city?" asked Luke.

"This I will not do," interrupted Paul. "I am a faithful son of Abraham."

"So be it. Nonetheless, this is what we, the elders of the assembly in Jerusalem, ask of you. No, Paul, this is what we *urge* you to do. You were here once before, with young Timothy . . ."

Timothy interrupted. "True, Paul was once here in this city with me, but I am now in my late twenties. I will soon be thirty. Would everyone please stop calling me *young!*" he growled.

Everyone laughed, and at a moment when laughter was sorely needed.

"You were here a few years ago with Timothy," the elder repeated, smiling. "At that time you had come from Greece and were under a Jewish vow. Your head was shaved. At the altar in the Temple you fulfilled your vow. This incident has led to our present suggestion to you.

"Here is what we ask: Shave your head. Take that vow again. Further, there are *four* men here in Jerusalem who also wish to take a vow *but* are too poor . . . that is, they cannot afford to pay for the expensive offerings that go with this vow. You are aware of the Jewish custom that can solve this problem of the poor wishing to take this vow?"

Paul nodded and then looked over toward his Gentile friends.

"The custom is this: A rich Jew shows his devotion to the Law by offering to pay the expenses of those who are too poor to take this vow."

"A rich Jew!" responded Sopater, as he threw up his hands in mock amazement. "I have been sitting here wondering how Paul could pay for his *own* vow!"

"We will find the money," mocked Aristarchus. "We will borrow it from Gaius, the rich Phrygian."

"We have heard rumors about these eight heathens you have been training," said one of the Jerusalem elders. "It appears the rumors are true!"

"Please be understanding," responded Paul, with a heavy sigh. "They are all that God gave me, proving beyond any doubt that God loves the Jews best."

Again, a moment of much needed levity. (All but James smiled at this warm-hearted teasing. James *never* smiled.)

Returning to the subject, one of the elders continued: "Paul, if you will pay for the offering of these four men, perhaps it will help the populace of Jerusalem to see that you are still devoted to the Law."

"I will do it," replied Paul with finality.

"Then let it be done!" said another of the elders. "But Paul, we cannot guarantee that this is enough. The Daggermen want you dead, no matter what."

"The last time I was here I had my hair cut off. Consequently not a single person recognized me. It seems the best way I can hide myself is to simply shave my head."

A quick discussion followed: "Where are we going to find the money to pay for *five* offerings?"

Mary and Mnason resolved the matter quickly.

The Jerusalem elders took time that night to receive the money sent by the Gentile churches. The Gentile brothers who had been chosen as messengers from the Gentile churches presented their letters to the elders. The letters stated the amount of money each church had sent. The brothers then presented the money to the elders. They, in turn, counted the money, verifying that the amount stated in the letter matched the amount given. And the amount given was no less than awesome. That fact was well noted by the Jewish elders.

But was it worth the cost—the cost being no less than Paul's life?! (I can say yes, but I could never have done so until years later. When? I saw the sovereignty of it all, in years to come, when I watched the emperor's army march out of Rome, bound for Israel, to destroy Jerusalem. It was at that time the Jewish believers fled into Galatia, Greece, and Asia Minor, and when they settled in a city, it was a *Gentile* church they became a part of!)

One last sack was opened that night. Paul presented to the elders the letter from the church that gathered in Corinth, along with the gift. Quietly, James said: "Brother Paul, we need not count this. You know that."

"Brother James, of all the gifts given, this one is the most important to be counted."

James nodded. And so the amount of money was counted. It corresponded with the amount stated in the letter from Corinth. The letter held the signatures of hundreds of believers! It was, along with the Philippian gift, the largest gift of all.

There was a brief prayer and the meeting ended.

As the eight brothers stepped out into Mary's courtyard, Paul, shifting to a brighter subject, told them about Peter's imprisonment, his miraculous delivery by an angel, and how he had come to this very gate and knocked.

"A little girl named Rhoda came out, saw Peter, and ran back into the house. No one would believe her words until they themselves saw Peter. And that was despite the fact that even as Peter was knocking at the gate they were all praying for his miraculous release!

"You are standing on the very ground where all this took place."

Secundus's eyes glistened as he reached down and took a pebble from the ground.

A few hours later a few of the Twelve met the *Eight*. The Eight were euphoric. The Twelve were not particularly impressed . . . not until many years later when they heard of the daring, the courage, and the power exhibited by those eight men. Nor could they ignore the fact that these Gentile church planters had raised up the ecclesia of God *all over* the Roman Empire and that those new churches were strong and Christ-centered. (And, even later, that most of these Gentile church planters died *before* the Twelve died, and they all died bravely.)

Paul had accomplished two things that memorable night. He had presented to the church in Jerusalem an amazingly large gift. Later, every person who would be helped by that money would know that it had come from *uncircumcised* believers! Even those who were called by that strange nickname . . . Christians.

The other accomplishment? Tomorrow, at the request of the elders, Paul would take a Jewish vow. Soon devout Jews all over the city would know that Paul was at least acting like a true follower of the Mosaic covenant.

Did Paul know he was only hours from virtually certain death? Tomorrow Paul would move out of Mnason's house and enter the Temple, *and* in so doing, his enemies would find him.

CHAPTER 24

The next morning Paul's company received a shock. "You are *very* disguised, indeed," observed Aristarchus, touching the top of his own head.

"Your sister would not recognize you . . . nor your young nephew," observed Timothy.

"Blastinius could fall on top of you and not know you," Trophimus added.

"Timothy, take the brothers around the city. During this next week I must live in the Temple area with the other four men who are taking the vow. As to Jerusalem, it is important that you brothers understand that this city is a shadow, a prefigurement of the ecclesia. It is, in fact, like a prophecy, a miniature, a picture of the church.

"Much has happened in this ancient city. You must see it and understand. Later, when you proclaim Christ, you can declare that all the things you saw here were pictures . . . pictures that have now been fulfilled in Christ and in his assembly."

A few minutes later, the young men departed for the streets of Jerusalem, and Paul went to the Temple. Timothy, tutored by Paul a few years earlier, did marvelously well in introducing his friends to Jerusalem . . . and to an understanding of her spiritual, unseen counterpart.

Later that day they saw Paul again. They met him in the Gentile courtyard. There he began explaining many things about the Temple that had meaning for believing Gentiles.

"For instance," he illustrated, "this wall is a divider. Gentiles cannot go beyond it; only Jews can. But in the *true* Jerusalem that wall has been ripped down by the cross of Christ. In *that* Jerusalem there is no wall."

While Paul was speaking, a friend of Blastinius's recognized Paul. He rushed out of the court and headed straight for Blastinius.

"Watch him closely," said Blastinius. "You must catch him in some unlawful act. When you do, scream to high heaven."

Unknown to Paul, for the rest of that day and for the rest of that week, he was followed.

The man also kept a close eye on Paul's friends, studying their features closely, hoping Paul would take them beyond the wall.

CHAPTER 25

Paul and his four Jewish companions made their home in a tiny corner of the Temple courtyard. The five men lived in that small space until the last day of the Pentecost feast, which would mark the end of their purification ritual.

The five men rose early that last day and entered the Temple. They lined up in a row and faced the Temple altar. Each had a sack in his hand, and in each sack, their shaved hair. (Paul had purchased two rams, a sheep, a basket of unleavened cakes, and a measure of wine for each man. Before that he had already paid for their lodging during their stay in Jerusalem.)

Paul, the man who had written the Galatian letter, had submitted to an ancient Hebrew vow . . . knowing full well he was free from all law and owed no debt to man or Temple. Truly, he was a man who could fit any season.

The vow was coming to its end. But one of Blastinius's spies thought that one of the men with Paul was Trophimus . . . an uncircumcised Greek; and he thought Paul had brought Trophimus into the Temple in order to desecrate it.

Such was the thinking of a man who had heard so many distorted stories that it had twisted his mind. He saw Paul only as a man bent on wickedness.

It is ironic that Paul had planned to depart Jerusalem the very next day. But suddenly, in that moment, his life was forever changed.

"It is Paul! . . . Paul! . . . Paul the destroyer of our sacred customs! Paul the blasphemer has brought a Gentile into the Temple! Paul has defiled the Temple!" So the spy thought, and so he screamed.

The crowd heard only three or four words, but that was all that was needed to hear: "Gentile . . . blasphemer . . . Paul . . . defiler!"

That which the Romans had hoped would not happen during this week of Pentecost suddenly did happen: A full-blown riot!

The encircling crowd grabbed Paul, dragged him out of the Temple, and began throwing rocks at him. In that horrible moment Paul was cursed, kicked, struck, and beaten. Paul's only thought was, *This crowd is growing, and I have only a few moments to live.*

But he then heard the unmistakable sound of Roman soldiers running toward the rioters. Soldiers had been stationed at almost every corner of the city's streets. The commotion could not have gone unnoticed. It therefore took only seconds for the soldiers to reach Paul. If Paul's Roman citizenship ever served him, it was to be in that hour.

The commander of the Roman garrison was a man named Lysias. (His title was *chiliarch*, that is, "the colonel of a thousand.") Lysias himself was soon rushing out of the Citadel of Antonio toward the Temple area. "Some poor soul," he muttered, "being beaten to death, or is it a planned insurrection? The Egyptian perhaps?" he growled.

Two hundred soldiers followed Lysias as he rushed through the street. It was a mercy of God that the fortress was just northwest of the Temple. A moment later Lysias and his soldiers were pushing their way through the rioters. Nevertheless, even though only moments had lapsed, untold damage had been inflicted on Paul's oft-beaten body.

What Lysias did next was what Roman soldiers were trained to do:

"Put that man in chains!" he ordered, as the soldiers pulled Paul out of the hands of the rioters. "What is the cause of this?" demanded Lysias. No clear answer was forthcoming. "Take this man to the citadel! Find out what he did. Beat it out of him."

Lysias did not know it, but he had saved Paul's life by no more than seconds. The Daggermen were even then pushing their way toward Paul. Only Roman blades stopped them.

Seeing the fury on the faces of the crowd, Lysias himself even joined in pulling Paul toward the staircase that led up to the citadel.

The mob was growing larger and more menacing *and* was still pushing forward. Instantly a chant arose from the crowd: "Kill him, kill him!"

Lysias barked to his soldiers, "Quick, pick him up and carry him to the citadel."

Lysias then yelled at Paul, "Egyptian! We have you this time."

(An Egyptian had recently tried to lead an uprising against the Romans, telling everyone to carry a dagger and to kill *any* Roman they found alone. Rumor had it that this Egyptian was in the city, that he had hundreds of followers, and that he was calling everyone to rally to him on the top of the Mount of Olives. From there, the rumor went, the Egyptian would lead a war against Rome.)

Paul later told me that what passed through his mind when he heard himself being referred to as Egyptian was, *I had no idea I was that dark skinned!*

Just as the citadel doors opened to receive the soldiers, Paul was lowered to the ground.

"May I speak to you?" choked Paul, in Greek.

"You speak Greek?" asked an astonished Lysias. "Are you not the Egyptian? How could you know Greek? And how did you know I understood Greek?"

"By your name," said Paul. "It is Greek. And, no, I am not an Egyptian. I am a Hebrew—I come from the city of Tarsus in Cilicia."

Lysias stared at the bloody face of a man so battered that he could hardly recognize him as human.

"Tarsus?" said Lysias, unbelieving.

"Yes," slurred Paul, "I am a citizen of *no mean city*." ("No mean city" was a term used by Euripides a century before. Only a very educated man would have been aware of this obscure quotation. Lysias *did* know the quote and marveled that Paul also knew it.)

"May I speak to the people?" asked Paul.

Incredibly, inexplicably, Lysias nodded.

Paul turned to the mob below and raised his hand. The screams subsided. Lysias received yet another surprise . . . this Jew not only knew Greek and Hebrew, this man was now addressing the crowd in the local Aramaic dialect.

Lysias had no idea what Paul was saying. It was enough just to see that the man could stand and speak.

Hearing their local dialect being spoken, the crowd grew quiet. Paul knew his audience and shaped his sentences to the moment.

"Brothers," Paul cried out in Aramaic, "hear my *defense*." Jews *had* to listen to a man who was defending himself in the face of death. It was an ancient and venerated Hebrew tradition.

"I am a Hebrew—from Tarsus, in Cilicia—but I have also

lived here in this city. It is here that I sat at the feet of *Gamaliel!* It was here in Jerusalem I learned the strictest interpretation of the law of our fathers. I was zealous for God, just as zealous as you are today."

Lysias was in awe; the crowd stood in rapt attention.

"I persecuted those who were called the followers of the Way. I persecuted them even to death. I put them in chains and delivered them to prison . . . women as well as men. I had the backing of the elders and the high priest. Your leaders can witness to this. Further, I received from their hands a letter to go to our brothers in Damascus and hunt down the followers of the Way in that city."

Paul knew, at some point, he would say something that would incite the crowd. Until then, Paul meant to take full advantage of the moment to speak of Christ.

He went on to tell of his encounter with the Lord Jesus Christ, of being struck blind, of Ananias's doubts, and of his baptism. Paul's voice cracked as he mentioned the death of Stephen . . . and finally, the telling sentence. He recounted the Lord's words to him: *"I will send you far away—to the Gentiles."*

It was the word *Gentile* that did it.

The screams began again: "Kill him, kill him! He is not fit to be alive! Away with him!"

The streets of Jerusalem were once again echoing with the same words that had been uttered against Jesus.

The mob pushed toward the Roman guards. Paul's life hung in the balance. Somewhere in the crowd a *sicarii* meant to tilt that balance.

CHAPTER 26

A dagger, with deadly accuracy, hurled through the air, its sure end Paul's heart. But effortlessly, a well-trained Roman guard lifted his shield and deflected the dagger. It fell harmlessly on the stone stairs.

Lysias pushed Paul through the gate of the citadel. As he did, the crowd began throwing dust on their heads. After the gate clanged shut, Paul found himself standing in near darkness. His body began to shake and spasm violently.

"Who are you? What did you say? Why this mob?"

Paul was attempting to control himself enough to answer when he heard, "To the torture chamber!"

Instantly, what was left of Paul's clothing was being stripped away. Paul knew exactly what awaited him. He would be chained by his hands, suspended in the air, and then whipped.

"The flagellum!"

Some dared call it worse than crucifixion. Not everyone survived. Those who do survive are usually left with irreparable damage to their body and, often, to their inward parts.

Paul had always been loath to save himself from similar situations by announcing his Roman citizenship . . . but not this time. Just as they were about to hoist him into the air, Paul asked the soldier nearest him: "Tell me, is it legal for you to flog a Roman citizen? Especially a Roman citizen who has not yet been found guilty of anything?"

The words "Roman citizen" stopped the proceedings. The soldier holding the flagellum dropped it. The soldier waiting to write down Paul's confession stepped back.

"Hold! Let me find Lysias."

A moment later an ashen soldier stammered, "This man is a Roman citizen."

Startled, Lysias stood and rushed to the chamber, mulling the consequences of his actions as he ran. Seeing Paul's much-scarred back, Lysias had yet another thought: *Perhaps this man is nothing but a liar.*

"You are a Roman citizen?" he whispered in Paul's ear.

"I am," said Paul, with what sounded like his dying breath. Something in Paul's voice assured Lysias that Paul was telling the truth.

"Loose this man." He then turned back to Paul. "I am also a Roman citizen. I paid a great deal of money for the privilege."

"The day I was born I was a Roman citizen!" said Paul.

Lysias swallowed hard. "Find this man clothes, and get a doctor immediately. Put him in a place of safekeeping."

"I have my own doctor. He is always with me when I travel. I saw him in the crowd. Find *him.*"

Lysias was dismayed . . . *his own doctor!* The soldiers led Paul to a cell, but were careful to leave the door unlocked, adding. "We have placed you in this cell *only* for your safekeeping."

That moment marked the beginning of nearly five years that Paul would remain a prisoner of the Roman Empire.

On the morrow, the Romans took desperate action to prevent the assassination of this particular Roman citizen.

CHAPTER 27

To the Sanhedrin with you." Paul looked up. A Temple guard was glaring at him. "It is the will of the procurator and the will of the Sanhedrin. Follow me, troublemaker." Temple guards were definitely *not* Roman guards.

Paul was uneasy as he stepped into the crowded streets of Jerusalem. He thought, *I am being taken into the very room where Jesus Christ stood some twenty-eight years ago. It is only fair, I suppose. It is the same room I dragged Christians into, to be beaten and imprisoned.*

It is also the room where the Twelve had appeared before the Sanhedrin and been threatened. Indeed, Jewish leaders seem to have a low tolerance for troublemakers, thought Paul.

I wonder if Blastinius will be there. Or the Daggermen? Paul thought as he carefully searched the room. There was a persistent rumor that the sicarii had once done business with Festus. At Festus's request, the *sicarii* had gone so far as to assassinate a former high priest!

There were many faces in the room Paul did not recognize. Their rural dress betrayed them—yes, the *sicarii* were present.

One of the leaders of the Sanhedrin rose and began reading a letter from Lysius. "I have requested that the Sanhedrin gather so as to clearly discover what charges they have against this man from Tarsus."

With that, Paul was escorted to the center of the room. There were no chains, but Temple guards stood on either side of him. (Lysias, a Gentile, was allowed only to listen to the proceedings from an anteroom.)

Seventy-one judges now stared down at Paul.

I wonder how many of these men were in this room twenty-eight years ago when my Lord was condemned to death. How many still live who sought to put Peter to death eighteen years ago? thought Paul.

Paul shifted his weight to one heel and began turning slowly in a full circle, thereby taking in the full view of the entire room.

At that moment a man named Ananias motioned for the proceedings to begin. By reputation Ananias had one of the worst records of any man ever to hold the office of high priest. By custom it was the place for someone else, besides Paul, to speak first. But Paul, as reported by Luke, seized the moment:

> "Brothers, I have always lived before God in all good conscience!"

Paul then heard an indistinct order coming from somewhere in the room. Suddenly one of the court ushers struck him hard across the mouth.

> Paul said to him, "God will slap you, you whitewashed wall! What kind of judge are you to break the law yourself by ordering me struck like that?"
>
> Those standing near Paul said to him, "Is that the way to talk to God's high priest?"

Paul was genuinely surprised, or at least he *looked* surprised. He lowered his voice and replied,

> "I'm sorry, brothers. I didn't realize he was the high priest. . . . for the Scriptures say, 'Do not speak evil of anyone who rules over you.'"

Paul found himself on the defensive—for him, a *rare* place indeed. But he quickly turned the situation back to his advantage. He knew the room was half-filled with *Pharisees* who believe in the resurrection of the dead, while the other half present were *Sadducees*, a people who do not believe in the resurrection of the dead nor in the existence of angels. He cried out:

> "Brothers, I am a Pharisee, as were all my ancestors! And I am on trial because my hope is in the resurrection of the dead!"

There is nothing so powerful—or divisive—as theological opinions. Suddenly Paul's detractors became his champions. The room erupted into arguments, insults, and finger shaking.

> Some of the teachers of religious law who were Pharisees jumped up to argue that Paul was all right. "We see nothing wrong with him," they shouted. "Perhaps a spirit or an angel spoke to him."

The Sadducees were enraged! (This included the high priest, himself a Sadducee.)

Meanwhile, Lysias could clearly discern the sudden change in the tone of men's voices. Remembering the riot of a few days earlier, he motioned to his soldiers to pull Paul to safety.

"Back to the citadel!"

"What am I going to say about this man?" Lysias was heard to grumble.

More quickly than he could grasp, Paul found himself back in his cell.

That night a group of Pharisees met together with an assortment of some of the most dangerous men in all of Israel. (The high priest, Ananias, was among those present.) Murder was on everyone's minds. Ananias, a master at the art, fanned the flames of hate. Years earlier he had led a delegation of Jews all the way to Rome, there to prove to the emperor that the Jewish nation had not been a party to an uprising against Rome led by a renegade, Eleazer Ben Dinai. Ananias had also bribed the former governor, Cumanus, so as to have some of Dinai's followers released from prison.

Now, on this particular night, Ananias had brought in the *sicarii* and the Zealots. Also present were men who were followers of Gischala, who had been killed while attempting to lead a revolt against Rome.

Nonetheless, everyone knew it was the *sicarii* who were the most influential revolutionaries in Israel at that moment. They even had close ties with a group of priests who had followed Eleazer Ben Dinai. To say the least, it was an impressive gathering of men of dark deeds.

Before the evening ended, Ananias had managed to bind these men to one idea: Kill Paul! An oath to that end was solemnly sworn . . . by no less than *forty* men. The oath? To neither eat nor drink until Paul was dead, which gave them no more than *three days* to kill Paul. Secrecy was taken for granted. The Pharisees, especially, had no fear that the plot would be disclosed, for they were in some ways as secretive in their dark decisions as were the *sicarii*.

No one in that room, however, remembered that the wife of one of those Pharisees was no less than the *sister* of Paul of Tarsus. This sister had a son, who in turn . . .

I must see Paul," insisted the young boy.

At first, simply because of his youth, the guards gave the boy no attention—not until they heard the words, "There is a plot to kill Paul."

One of the soldiers quickly ushered the boy into the presence of the captain of the guard, who in turn escorted the boy to Paul's cell. There Paul and Lysius listened. "Don't be afraid. And take your time," said Lysius gently.

"Forty men have taken an oath—many of them *sicarii*—to kill Paul . . . *tomorrow.*" The boy caught his breath and continued. "In the morning you will receive a request from the Sanhedrin to have Paul returned to the Hall of Polished Stones. The Sanhedrin will tell you they wish to ask Paul more questions. Instead, the forty will fall upon Paul on the way to the hall. Forty men, sir, and they are all prepared to die . . . as they throw themselves against your Roman soldiers. Anything, in order to reach Paul with a knife."

Turning to his mother's brother, the boy added: "Uncle Paul, they have taken an oath, some sort of religious oath. My mother explained it to me—it is a very serious, very solemn oath. They have vowed not to eat any food or to drink any water until you are dead. But not only that, they have placed themselves under a *curse*. Uh, that means, if they fail to kill you, they have asked God to pour his wrath upon them and curse them."

Paul blew out a long breath. "Mmm, a vow to the death! A curse upon themselves!" Paul looked up at Lysias: "This they will do."

Lysias did not hesitate. He turned to his guards, "Let them starve to death, and let them die of thirst. No man will take *my* prisoners."

Late that evening, *two hundred* infantrymen surrounded Paul and marched him outside the city. Then, just outside the gate, they were met by another *two hundred* spearmen plus another *seventy* soldiers on horseback. In the midst of them all, Paul. And even then they had disguised him as a Roman soldier and placed him on a horse!

The entire troop of four hundred and seventy heavily armed soldiers moved west toward Caesarea. When they reached a place called Antipatris, the infantry returned to Jerusalem. From that point on, it was *only* seventy mounted Roman soldiers who escorted Paul through the Judean plains and on to Caesarea!

So it came to pass that our dear brother Paul—who only hours before had been a prisoner in Jerusalem—was led into the capital city of Caesarea, and into the Praetorium, the governor's palace.

The governor's name was Antonius Felix. (Twenty-two years earlier, that same office had been held by one Pontius Pilate.)

As he entered the Praetorium, Paul could not help but mutter, "Now shall I see Felix. They have a saying about him: Felix exercises the power of a king, with the mind of a slave. I wonder what fate shall be mine under this, my newest captor. I know only this: His reputation is as bad as that of his predecessor,

Ventidius Cumanus. But this I also know: My Lord has promised that I shall see Rome and that *I shall* stand before Nero."

The seventy cavalrymen dismounted, and Paul was led inside like some regal visitor. Paul smiled, and then chuckled as he thought, *How little did my father know what he was doing for me when he was made a Roman citizen.*

Now that you have this information, I, Priscilla, feel it important that you know just who Antonius Felix was. Shortly before the emperor Claudius died, he appointed Felix as governor of Judea. The appointment had come about for one reason only: Felix had a brother in the Roman court, named Pallas. The main business of Pallas was to flatter Claudius. Pallas was also a friend of Claudius's wife, as well as a friend to her child by an earlier marriage . . . *Nero.* When Nero took the throne at age sixteen, Pallas became one of Nero's chief advisors.

Felix's job was simple. He was in Caesarea-by-the-Sea to do two things. The first was to keep the strong Roman heel on the restless Jewish population. Second, he was somehow expected to curry the favor of the Jews. This was no small task.

(Felix did not know it, but on the day he met Paul he had less than two years left as governor of Judea. His reign would end because of the outbreak of a riot in Caesarea. When that happened, Felix would be called back to Rome, an utter failure. The only reason Nero did not behead Felix was that Pallas intervened for his life.)

Felix was handed the letter sent to him by Lysius. The contents were not to Felix's liking. He now had a man on his hands who was both a Roman citizen and a controversial Jew. It was obvious the Jews hated this man. It was equally obvious that Felix had to not only protect Paul, but give him a fair hearing.

Soon after Paul's arrival in Caesarea, the Sanhedrin also arrived. With them was a lawyer they had hired, Tertullus by name. He was a famous, highly skilled attorney, hired by no less than Ananias. His job: to inflict as much damage on Paul's character as possible. Beyond that, Felix *owed* Ananias a favor.

(Eight years earlier, at the time of the uprising led by Eleazer Ben Dinai, Ananias had played a central role in having one of Felix's enemies, a man named Jonathan, assassinated.) Yes, Felix owed Ananias, and Ananias had come to collect.

Here is the letter that Lysias sent to Felix. (Luke, who moved to Caesarea to be with Paul while Paul was in prison there, obtained a copy of this letter.)

> "From Claudius Lysias, to his Excellency, Governor Felix. Greetings! This man was seized by some Jews, and they were about to kill him when I arrived with the troops. When I learned that he was a Roman citizen, I removed him to safety. Then I took him to their high council to try to find out what he had done. I soon discovered it was something regarding their religious law—certainly nothing worthy of imprisonment or death. But when I was informed of a plot to kill him, I immediately sent him on to you. I have told his accusers to bring their charges before you."

Ananias demanded that Felix allow a public hearing. Using a famous Roman lawyer guaranteed that the hearing would be conducted by strict Roman protocol. Felix agreed.

Paul was ushered into one of the large rooms within the palace. He surveyed the room. Yes, there was Blastinius, and yes, there were the *sicarii*. Taking a moment of grim satisfaction, Paul muttered out loud: "None starved to death it seems."

Tertullus rose.

He knew that Felix had been born a slave and had risen to power through the influence of his brother, Pallas. Tertullus's strategy was to appeal to Felix's ego. Because Luke was also one of the people present in the room that day, we know Tertullus's speech in its entirety:

"Your Excellency, you have given peace to us Jews and have enacted reforms for us. And for all of this we are very grateful to you. But lest I bore you, kindly give me your attention for only a moment as I briefly outline our case against this man. For we have found him to be a troublemaker, a man who is constantly inciting the Jews throughout the world to riots and rebellions against the Roman government. He is a ringleader of the sect known as the Nazarenes. Moreover he was trying to defile the Temple when we arrested him. You can find out the truth of our accusations by examining him yourself."

Felix, listening to Tertullus rather casually, motioned for Paul to respond. Nor did it miss Felix's eye that Paul was the most relaxed person in the room.

Paul concentrated his defense on one very simple point: There had been a riot in Jerusalem, but he was guilty of no wrongdoing.

Paul said, "I know, sir, that you have been a judge of Jewish affairs for many years, and this gives me confidence as I make my defense. You can quickly discover that it was no more than twelve days ago that I arrived in Jerusalem to worship at the Temple. I didn't argue with anyone in the Temple, nor did I incite a riot in any synagogue or on the streets of the city. These men certainly cannot prove the things they accuse me of doing.

"But I admit that I follow the Way, which they call a sect. I worship the God of our ancestors, and I firmly believe the Jewish law and everything written in the books of prophecy. I have hope in God, just as these men do, that he will raise both the righteous and the ungodly. Because of this, I always try to maintain a clear conscience before God and everyone else.

"After several years away, I returned to Jerusalem with money to aid my people and to offer sacrifices to God. My accusers saw me in the Temple as I was completing a purification ritual. There was no crowd around me and no rioting. But some Jews from the province of Asia were there—and they ought to be here to bring charges if they have anything against me! Ask these men here what wrongdoing the Jewish high council found in me, except for one thing I said when I shouted out, 'I am on trial before you today because I believe in the resurrection of the dead!' "

Paul was seeking to demonstrate to Felix that this whole affair was nothing more than a theological disagreement.

Felix sat quietly as Paul spoke. It was becoming clear to him that he was facing a serious dilemma. He needed to placate the Jews, but at the same time he did not dare place a Roman citizen in jeopardy unfairly. If he made a misstep here he knew his position as governor might suddenly be in jeopardy. That jeopardy had a name: Nero.

Felix's solution was predictable. He decided to stall. To everyone's surprise Felix suddenly dismissed the meeting. There were grumbles, complaints, and a few obscenities as Felix walked out of the room. No one there that day could imagine that Felix would take no action on this case for two more years.

As Paul was led out of the room he was not sure whether to laugh or to cry. He had seen Blastinius, the *sicarii, and* the high priest . . . defeated. On the other hand, he was not looking forward to a long confinement in prison. Somehow he knew he must try to find a way to be released from the Caesarean imprisonment. But no such way was ever found.

A few days later Felix came with his wife, Drusilla, who was Jewish. Sending for Paul, they listened as he told them about faith in Christ Jesus. As he reasoned with them about righteousness and self-control and the judgment to come, Felix was terrified. "Go away for now," he replied. "When it is more convenient I'll call for you again." He also hoped that Paul would bribe him, so he sent for him quite often and talked with him.

Paul offered no bribes but gladly shared the good news of Jesus Christ with Felix.

During the following two years Paul had two very close companions. One was Aristarchus, the other Luke. The Eight all remained in Caesarea for several months, hoping for Paul's early release.

(Eventually Paul sent them back into the Gentile world to care for the churches, but always adding, "If you hear that I am about to be released, come to me quickly.")

The next spring, which was twenty-nine years after the resurrection of Jesus Christ, a riot broke out in Caesarea. Because of that riot, Nero called Felix back to Rome. The new governor whom Nero appointed was a man named Porcius Festus.

Even before Festus arrived in Israel, the religious leaders of Israel let Festus know that resolving the issue of Paul should be his first priority. Festus responded. Even before settling at Caesarea, he went straight to Jerusalem to hear the Jews' charges against Paul. Like Felix he immediately began looking for a compromise solution. But the high priest let it be known that he would be wise to please the Hebrew leaders by turning Paul back into their hands.

Festus had one advantage over Felix: he owed the high priest no favors. On the other hand, the high priest's plan had not changed: Get Paul near Jerusalem. The *sicarii* would do the rest.

It was not to be. Instead, Festus invited the Jewish leaders to come once more to Caesarea. They accepted.

Festus's very first public hearing had to do with none other than our brother Paul. Now, for the second time, Paul stood before the justice of Judea. And once more the Jewish leaders, in bringing their charges against Paul, made it sound like Paul was a threat to the entire world. But also once more, the charges were vague. Worst of all, there were no witnesses.

Festus was frustrated. He turned to his counselors. But even they could say nothing to enlighten him in this matter. One thing was very clear—these Jewish leaders had no real case against Paul. And when Paul was brought into the room to make his defense, that is exactly what he said:

> "I am not guilty. . . . I have committed no crime against the Jewish laws or the Temple or the Roman government."
>
> Then Festus, wanting to please the Jews, asked him, "Are you willing to go to Jerusalem and stand trial before me there?"

It was a crafty move on the part of Festus. The Jewish leaders smiled.

Paul hesitated. He faced a heavy dilemma. He did not wish to stay in prison any longer, but he knew certain death awaited him in Jerusalem. His *only* way out was to appeal to Caesar. Few men ever dared do that. To appeal to Caesar meant the possibility of languishing in a Roman prison for years, awaiting Caesar's pleasure. The hesitation ended. Paul preferred prison in Rome over giving his enemies the satisfaction of killing him.

> Paul replied, "No! This is the official Roman court, so I ought to be tried right here. You know very well I am not guilty. If I have done something worthy of death, I don't refuse to die. But if I am innocent, neither you nor anyone else has a right to turn me over to these men to kill me."

Paul swallowed hard and, knowing full well he was sentencing himself to a very long time in a prison in Rome, announced:

> "I appeal to Caesar!"

Felix, hearing this legal pronouncement, responded with a legal pronouncement:

> "Very well! You have appealed to Caesar, and to Caesar you shall go!"

Those words settled it! Paul would stand before the emperor of Rome who alone would decide his fate. The only advantage Paul won that day was to lend maddening frustration to his enemies.

Was his stay in Caesarea over? Not quite! It would take time to do the legal processing. (Luke immediately sent word to the Eight to return to Caesarea.) But there was also another delay before Paul's departure for Rome.

Paul had stood before the rulers of Israel. (Before his life ended he had also stood before *three* Roman governors and the emperor.) Before leaving Israel he would stand before Jewish royalty . . . the grandson of Herod the Great.

CHAPTER 29

"A state visitor! *Royal* visitors!" mused Festus. "Just how long will it be before Agrippa and his sister Bernice arrive?"

"Ten days," replied his adviser.

"Agrippa rules the land of Galilee does he not? And is it not this land from which sprang the prophet Jesus?"

"Yes, and it was Agrippa's father who tried to extinguish this cult even while it was being born. He did end the life of Jesus' cousin. But as to the cult, he was unsuccessful. The leaders of this sect kept escaping whenever Herod Agrippa had them imprisoned."

Festus laughed. "Would that it were so easy for me to deal with this Roman Jew. Or should I say this Jewish Roman?

"Does this mean, then, that Agrippa II could provide me with insight into these strange practices the Jews observe?"

"Yes, your Excellency! Agrippa and his sister are both proselytes of the Jewish religion," said the adviser.

"Good! Then I shall see to it that when Agrippa is present I speak to him of Paul. I cannot understand half of what he, or the other Jews, are saying to me. Their religion baffles me.

"Tell me, exactly what part of Israel does Agrippa rule?"

"An area called Chalcis, your Excellency," replied his

adviser. "A small area lying between the mountains of Lebanon and a mountain called Hermon. Of late the size of his domain has been increased."

"And his sister—tell me what you know of her."

"She is Bernice. She also has a sister, Druscilla. Druscilla is the wife of the deposed Felix. "I must add, Sir, that there are rumors that Bernice and King Agrippa II have an incestuous relationship."

"Is there proof?"

"None, sir."

"Then we shall ignore the rumor."

Ten days later, with great pomp and ceremony, Agrippa and his sister arrived in Caesarea. Festus spent most of the first day's visit asking questions about the Jewish religion. Eventually the subject turned to Paul.

"We have heard much about this man," said Agrippa. "He seems to be as much a nuisance to the religious Jews as was John the Baptist in the days of my father!" laughed Agrippa. "Let me be as foolish as my father and ask to interview this Paul. Perhaps I can lend you some insight as to what this controversy is really about."

"I would be most appreciative," responded Festus.

"You will stand before King Agrippa," Paul was informed. "Best you wear your finest clothes. You will be standing in the midst of a great deal of royal extravagance. It seems you will be the main event in Agrippa's visit with the governor."

"I will play my part," assured Paul. "I have been tried in the same courtroom as was my Lord. Why not stand before the son of the man who beheaded John the Baptist. How many such honors can my Lord bestow on me?"

Paul knew he would be given a time to speak, and Agrippa would then explain to Festus, as best he could, what this controversy was over.

In preparing for this hearing, Festus invited just about every important person in Caesarea, Jew or Gentile, to be present. Luke was one of those permitted to come.

It was in a room called the Hall of Audience that everyone gathered. Until the day when Paul would stand before Nero, this day was the most extravagant display of royalty Paul had witnessed. Bugles were blown, trumpets blared, drums rolled . . . then Festus, with his royal friends, entered. As one, the entire assembly rose and bowed.

Luke later observed: "I never saw Paul look so tiny as in that moment when he was ushered into the center of the room."

"King Agrippa, you and those present here today observe this man. The Jews have asked that I send him to Jerusalem to be tried. They wish, by their law, to somehow bring him to his death. I find that he has done nothing deserving death. As a citizen of the city of Rome he has appealed his case to our illustrious emperor, Nero. I have decided to accept his appeal. Paul shall go to Rome. There he will present his case to Caesar.

"But this is my quandary. I do not know what to write to Caesar concerning this man. Therefore, King Agrippa, I have asked you to hear this man, that you might advise me as to what I might say to Caesar.

"It seems to me it is unreasonable to send a prisoner to Rome, yet not be able to indicate what charges are laid against him," added Festus, in good humor. The audience laughed dutifully.

Agrippa, thirty-two years old, in the prime of life and at the zenith of his power, motioned to Paul and, with a hint of royal disdain, announced: "You have permission to speak for yourself."

Paul did exactly that.

"I am fortunate, King Agrippa, that you are the one hearing my defense against all these accusations made by the Jewish leaders, for I know you are an expert on Jewish customs and controversies. Now please listen to me patiently!

"As the Jewish leaders are well aware, I was given a thorough Jewish training from my earliest childhood among my own people and in Jerusalem. If they would admit it, they know that I have been a member of the Pharisees, the strictest sect of our religion. Now I am on trial because I am looking forward to the fulfillment of God's promise made to our ancestors. In fact, that is why the twelve tribes of Israel worship God night and day, and they share the same hope I have. Yet, O king, they say it is wrong for me to have this hope! Why does it seem incredible to any of you that God can raise the dead?

"I used to believe that I ought to do everything I could to oppose the followers of Jesus of Nazareth. Authorized by the leading priests, I caused many of the believers in Jerusalem to be sent to prison. And I cast my vote against them when they were condemned to death. Many times I had them whipped in the synagogues to try to get them to curse Christ. I was so violently opposed to them that I even hounded them in distant cities of foreign lands.

"One day I was on such a mission to Damascus, armed with the authority and commission of the leading priests. About noon, Your Majesty, a light from heaven brighter than the sun shone down on me and my companions. We all fell down, and I heard a voice saying to me in Aramaic, 'Saul, Saul, why are you persecuting me? It is hard for you to fight against my will. '

"'Who are you, sir?' I asked.

"And the Lord replied, 'I am Jesus, the one you are persecuting. Now stand up! For I have appeared to you to appoint you as my servant and my witness. You are to tell the world about this experience and about other times I will appear to you. And I will protect you from both your own people and the Gentiles. Yes, I am going to send you to the Gentiles, to open their eyes so they may turn from darkness to light, and from the power of Satan to God. Then they will receive forgiveness for their sins and be given a place among God's people, who are set apart by faith in me.'

"And so, O King Agrippa, I was not disobedient to that vision from heaven. I preached first to those in Damascus, then in Jerusalem and throughout all Judea, and also to the Gentiles, that all must turn from their sins and turn to God—and prove they have changed by the good things they do."

Paul paused and looked at Bernice. As a woman always in charge of her emotions, she showed no reactions whatsoever to Paul's words. He continued:

"Some Jews arrested me in the Temple for preaching this, and they tried to kill me. But God protected me so that I am still alive today to tell these facts to everyone, from the least to the greatest. I teach nothing except what the prophets and Moses said would happen—that the Messiah would suffer and be the first to rise from the dead as a light to Jews and Gentiles alike."

Festus found himself exactly where he had always been, utterly dismayed at this new vocabulary—death, resurrection, one God, *one* way . . . and many other statements that did not fit into his thoughts. Agrippa, on the other hand, was following every word.

Suddenly Festus, his mind no longer able to contain all this strange talk, shouted: "Paul, you are insane. Too much learning has made you mad!"

Agrippa was sincerely surprised at Festus's outburst. Further, in that moment Agrippa realized how truly untutored Festus was in the ways of the Hebrew people.

> "I am not insane, Most Excellent Festus. I am speaking the sober truth. And King Agrippa knows about these things. I speak frankly, for I am sure these events are all familiar to him, for they were not done in a corner! King Agrippa, do you believe the prophets?"

Paul paused, and then stated emphatically: "I *know* you do . . . "

Caught off guard for only an instant, Agrippa spoke words dressed in a condescending smile: "Paul, do you think you can make me a Christian so quickly?"

"Whether quickly or not," Paul responded, "I pray to God that both you and everyone in this audience might become the same as I am." Paul raised his arms and added, "Except for these chains!"

The audience found Paul's words and gesture humorous. All laughed, and some even broke into applause.

> Then the king, the governor, Bernice, and all the others stood and left.

Paul's audience had ended. Festus and Agrippa retired to a private place and carefully discussed the events of the hour. In essence, all Agrippa could do was agree with Festus.

"You are correct, Festus. This matter has absolutely nothing to do with Roman law. The man is innocent. This is all a matter of customs, religious teachings, and theology. The man has done nothing except make a few religious Jews angry. Again, he has broken no Roman laws."

Festus sighed. "And how can I explain *that* to a Roman emperor? He could have been released, if he had not appealed."

I, Priscilla, feel I must pause here to tell you the fate of these people.

Seven years later an uprising broke out, not in Caesarea or Jerusalem, but all across Israel. Agrippa and Bernice fled to Rome. Bernice became the mistress of a future emperor.

And Festus? At the time Festus took office, there was a group of zealots, followers of Eleazer Ben Dinai, who were causing trouble all over Israel. These men, along with the rising influence of the *sicarii*, caused Festus many problems. But there were forces even more powerful at work. Prophecies of apocalyptic proportions were being proclaimed everywhere in Israel. Festus spent his two years in office dealing with this and other unrelenting opposition. And whatever he did succeed in containing, he could not stop the prophecies, all of which spoke of impending doom. Everywhere, it seemed, some Hebrew was standing up to declare that he was a prophet or the deliverer of Israel. When Festus did succeed in putting down disorder in one place, it broke out in another.

Worst of all, Gentiles in Caesarea were claiming that they should control the city, while leading Jews made the same claim. From Rome, Nero decided in favor of the Greeks, causing the Hebrews in that city to lose their equality. As a result of the outrage that followed, Festus found himself losing his grip on his own destiny as well as that of Israel. So, after only two years, Festus was replaced by a procurator named Albinus, a man who was even more corrupt—and less prepared to rule Israel—than was Festus.

The power and glory that these people knew on the day they heard Paul soon faded into ignominy.

And Paul?

A few days after the hearing, Festus began preparations to have Paul shipped to Rome. Unknown to himself, Paul was

181

about to add yet another *two* years to his imprisonment . . . in Rome.

In just six more years, Israel went to war with Rome. But only four years after Paul had sailed from Caesarea, the Christians in Rome would either be put to death or flee Rome.

Paul had eight years to live. Jerusalem had ten years left before being leveled to the ground.

Now it is time for me, Priscilla, to begin to bring to an end my part in recounting this story to you. I will continue on to the time when Paul discovers that a ship he is being forced to board is bound for destruction. Beyond that point, I will leave it to another to complete this story.

Let us now join Paul as he prepares to board a ship waiting in the harbor at Caesarea.

Luke, do not take anything on this ship that can be ruined by water. Your book on the life of Christ . . . the two years of hard work you spent working on it in Caesarea . . . it can all be lost in a minute. Ships sink! Furthermore, it is late in the year for any ship to attempt to reach Rome. I have asked several brothers to meet me in Rome, but to go there by land. Give *them* your manuscripts."

"I have two copies," replied Luke. "I can afford to lose one. Besides, I am not sure anyone will be interested in this book. Mark and Matthew have already told the story of the Lord's life."

"Send *both* by land," implored Paul. "Furthermore, there may be as many as a hundred or more people who might desire to read a Gentile view of the Lord's life."

"Really?" replied an incredulous Luke.

"By the way," Paul continued, "I have been allowed one person to accompany me to Rome. I have requested two. The Romans granted my request this morning. Aristarchus will be traveling with us."

"Where is he? In fact, where are the Eight . . . uh, the seven?" asked Luke.

"They should all be arriving any moment. I dread hearing them tease Aristarchus."

Luke laughed: "They do not give one another much space, do they?

"Have you met your Roman escort?"

Paul said, "Yes. His name is Julius. He heads a small Roman garrison. He has informed me that this ship does not go all the way to Rome. *That* troubles me. I only hope we reach Rome—or a safe harbor—before the northeastern winds begin to blow. If the next ship we are on fights the northeastern winds, we will *not* make it to Rome.

"A number of the passengers on this ship, you might be interested to know, are criminals. Most are bound for death in Rome. Julius tells me that some will be sold in the marketplace, others will be fed to the lions, a few will be turned into gladiators. They will fight to the death in the Circus Maximus."

"Perhaps we will have the opportunity to speak to some of them about our Lord before we reach Rome," Luke responded. "Will you be kept with them?"

Paul answered, "No, I understand these prisoners will be chained, then taken below. Each will have his chains nailed to a large piece of timber in the hold of the ship. The Lord has delivered me from that fate. Once more my Roman citizenship has served me well. Festus has ordered that I be allowed the run of the deck . . . in chains of course."

"Then let us hope for fair weather," said Luke.

"*And* that we reach Rome before winter. If we do not, we will face the Etesian winds," added Paul, grimly. "Those winds almost took my life and the lives of Mark and Barnabas as well. They are winds of death. No man, no ship, should dare gamble against those winds."

Paul's young men arrived. And, yes, they were teasing Aristarchus, mostly disclosing their jealousy. Aristarchus was the strongest and the most audacious among the brothers, except, of course, for Gaius. That is why Paul chose him for the journey. He might have chosen Timothy, except for Timothy's frail health.

Suddenly there was the clatter of Roman chariots. Everyone, even Paul, was surprised to see Festus coming to the docks to bid Paul farewell. The truth was, Festus had grown to admire Paul. Festus's visit was brief. After he departed, nine men began bidding one another an affectionate farewell. When the teasing of Aristarchus began again, Paul intervened.

"The chance that you will be alive when Aristarchus, Luke, and I are dead is excellent. The season for sailing this sea is late—I have a strange foreboding about this voyage. The only thing that comforts me is that my Lord has promised that *I* should see Rome and that *I* should stand before Nero. When the Lord told me this, he did not make mention of Luke or Aristarchus!"

Everyone roared with laughter.

After that, Paul began his instructions for each man:

"Attempt to stay in touch with Gaius if at all possible. After all, Egypt is a long way from Rome and Israel. Also stay in touch with one another. When I have arrived in Rome, I will send a letter to all of you. I will be asking you to come to me as quickly as possible. I am aware that, at that time, you will each be involved in the Lord's work in numerous places. Come only if it does not jeopardize the Lord's work where you are.

"Timothy, you are to leave here and go immediately to Ephesus. Remain there until such time as you hear that I have arrived in Rome; then go *immediately* to Philippi. From there, come to Rome. You are the brother most traveled, therefore you are also the one best prepared to minister to the church in Rome, in my stead. If I die at the hands of Nero, I expect you to care for the assembly in Rome and Ephesus during the time those two churches pass through a period of transition.

"Secundus, I send you immediately to northern Greece. Tychicus, Trophimus; you are to move out into the area around Ephesus, and continue moving throughout all the province of Asia Minor. Visit each and every church in that province. You speak the language and the dialects of Asia Minor. Take full advantage of that fact, and spread the gospel by all means. Nor should you hesitate to plant other assemblies in other towns in that province."

Paul took a deep breath, studied the faces of Tychicus and Trophimus, and then added, "There is someone you must find. It is my strong opinion that there should be *nine* of you, not eight. If Epaphras is amenable, ask him to join you in the work."

Then Paul suddenly changed his mind: "No, that is not correct. Find Epaphras, yes. But when you hear I have reached Rome, send Epaphras to me."

"Epaphras is not a well-traveled man," answered Titus.

"That is true," said Paul. "But there is something that he is . . . he *is* Epaphras!"

Everyone laughed joyfully! And everyone understood. Epaphras was a unique human being, the depth of whose capacities had never been plumbed.

"Titus, you are to return to Syria. Visit the churches in Syria in the area lying outside Antioch. Travel throughout all Syria, and then into my home country, Cilicia. Tell all the churches what has transpired here. There is something else I want you to do, Titus: Go to Cyprus. Find Barnabas. Tell him everything that has happened these last two years. And discover for me, please, how the new Gentile assemblies on Cyprus are faring in the midst of the old Jewish assemblies. In other words, Titus, bring me news of all the assemblies in Cilicia, Syria, and

Cyprus. Furthermore, let me know if the gospel has reached Crete. If it has, find out if it was carried there by Jews or by Gentiles.

"Sopater, go to northern Greece, and report to Berea and Thessalonica what has happened in the last few months. Visit with the new assembly in Dyrrhachium and strengthen them. From time to time, go down to Corinth and encourage the brothers and sisters there.

"Now Luke has something to tell all of you."

For a moment Luke looked surprised, then his face flushed. You could see that he was a little hesitant.

"I have begun writing another book," said Luke.

At once the brothers cheered.

"What is the book about?" asked Timothy.

"Having finished the story of the Lord's life, I have decided to write the story of what happened after the Lord ascended. As you know, I have been here in Caesarea waiting for Paul to be released. While here, I have gathered a great deal of information about the Lord's life—much of it new—and then written it all down. But in the process, I have also learned a great deal about what happened after the Lord's ascension . . . and about Pentecost . . . er, up until the time Barnabas went to Antioch. I am now writing it all out in full."

"That is wonderful!" said Secundus. "But why stop at Antioch?"

"What do you mean?" asked Luke.

"Why not tell the story of what happened after Barnabas came to Antioch?"

"What story is that?" asked Paul.

Secundus looked mortified. "What story? *Your* story, Paul!"

"Absolutely not!" replied Paul. "Absolutely not. I am controversial enough. Besides, who would be interested. In fact, who would even care!"

"Brother Luke has all the power and gift to write the story in such a way that you would not appear to be controversial," urged Tychicus.

"The answer is *no!*"

In a loud whisper, Secundus rejoined: "Luke, maybe after he is dead. Then you will not need his permission."

On that humorous note the discussion ended. The time for the ship to cast off was near.

Exactly thirty years had passed since the resurrection of Jesus Christ and the birth of the church at Pentecost. It was August.

At that moment Julius appeared. "Who are these men?" asked Julius roughly, looking at those gathered with Paul. To his surprise, no one quailed under his glare.

"Friends," replied Paul.

With that, Julius relaxed his tone. "You are the only Roman citizen on this ship. I have been told by Festus to treat you with every favor, also your two companions. This I will do. I trust you will cause me no problems. If you do, you will end up in the ship's hold. It has been my duty for years to take criminals from this area of the world and bring them to Rome. Only on the rarest occasions have I escorted a criminal who is a Roman citizen. They have all behaved themselves well. I trust you will join that number."

"He is the gentlest man you shall ever meet," replied Secundus.

"He is also a man much loved," added Trophimus. "This is why he has been allowed a doctor to go with him and also a bodyguard."

Everyone turned and stared at Trophimus. Until that moment no one had thought of Aristarchus as a bodyguard.

"Will you join us, please, Julius, as we speak to our God?" asked Paul as he began to kneel. Julius was taken aback at Paul's words, and even more so as he watched all the men around him kneel. Julius did not kneel, but he did watch, and watch carefully. It was a telling moment. In the days ahead Julius would become a close friend of Paul of Tarsus. In fact, there would come a moment, on their *second* ship, when it would be Paul, not Julius, who would be in command of the journey.

From that moment, there on the docks of Caesarea, Paul never received a discourteous word from anyone on board ship.

After the prayer, Aristarchus turned to Julius: "Exactly what is your designation?"

"I am an Augustinian cohort—you might call me an imperial escort or courier. I travel with about a dozen soldiers under me. Criminals are placed into my hands. It is my task to then find a ship and safely transport the criminals to Rome. Most of these criminals see the end of their lives shortly after they reach Rome."

Julius turned toward the ship. "We will be traveling a coastal route. This ship originated in Adramyttium, which is east of Assos. When this ship reaches its destination, we will have to find another vessel that is bound for Rome. I expect that we will see Rome by the end of October."

"That is very close to the beginning of the Etesian winds, sir," observed Paul, in a voice that sounded of doom.

"We will avoid such winds," replied Julius. "Now, it is time for our departure. You men may come aboard with Paul for a moment, if you so desire."

The entire company mounted the gangplank. There were final hugs and tears, then a quick end as the ship caught a light westerly breeze. There was a hasty retreat to shore, then a few final shouts of encouragement.

A moment later, the ship turned northeast, its next port, Sidon, some sixty-seven miles away.

What happened in Sidon sealed Julius's admiration of Paul.

CHAPTER 3 1

Some one hundred or more believers stood on shore waiting to greet Paul as the ship neared Sidon. Their songs wafted on the autumn breeze. Many of the believers were waving palm branches, the traditional greeting of the Jewish people for those whom they revered.

The ship's call at Sidon was brief. When Aristarchus reboarded, he had joined the elite company of Mark and Timothy—that is, he was a brother loaded down with more food than anyone could ever hope to carry.

As the ship continued hugging the coastline, it approached the Tarsus mountains. Paul looked out upon his beloved homeland, Cilicia, for the last time ever.

For the next fifteen days the ship did not dock. As it passed the gulf of Attalia, Paul never took his eyes off the shore. When Luke realized that this was the very place where Paul had first disembarked for Galatia, he began pummeling Paul with questions about the details of his and Barnabas's arrival at the Attalia port.

The ship's next port was Myra. "This is no place to winter; the waters are too shallow," muttered Julius. A moment later he received good news. An Egyptian grain ship, bound for Rome, was anchored offshore.

Once Julius boarded the grain ship, both its captain and

owner gave way to his control. Julius would make the final decisions about everything that had to do with this voyage.

By the time Paul, Luke, Aristarchus, and the criminals boarded, there were a total of 278 souls on the ship. Though Paul had heard of ships that could hold up to a thousand people, he had never been on one that could hold 278 people *and* a shipload of wheat!

The prisoners were dutifully secured in the ship's hold. Paul and his two companions were allowed the run of the deck.

Julius stepped up to Paul's side. "We will sail past Rhodes and the southern tip of Greece. We should reach Brundisium, Italy, within ten to fifteen days. From there we will sail up the western side of Italy. Rome has two ports: Ostia and Port Augusti. A pilot will choose at which city we shall dock."

It was on September 16 that the huge grain ship pulled away from Myra. The winds were not favorable, so the ship moved slowly.

The ship continued almost due west, hugging the coastline of Asia Minor until they came to the town of Cnidus. (Just a few more miles and the ship would pass the mouth of the Aegean Sea, with Ephesus on one side and Corinth on the other.)

"From Cnidus we will sail along the southern coast of Crete, then out into the open seas until we come to the southern side of Sicily," the captain informed them.

Just as the ship moved out of Cnidus and into the choppy seas, it encountered strong head winds. Then the winds shifted. Suddenly the ship was being blown to the south side of Crete.

The last days of the season for *any* ship to sail the Mediterranean were ending.

About midway on the southern side of Crete was a town called Fair Havens.

"We cannot winter here. We would have to remain

anchored offshore all winter," said the captain. "A strong wind will drive us to the shore."

"I agree," said Julius. "If we stay here we will have to spend the entire winter on board this ship, which would drive every one of us mad. Nor would I put it past the prisoners to mutiny. There is only one thing to do: sail to the western tip of Crete. There is a very good port at the city of Phoenix. It is only forty miles from here. We can winter there."

It sounded so simple and so safe, *until* this word reached the ears of Paul.

"You must winter *here*, at Fair Havens. You can take all the passengers to shore in the dinghy. You must not attempt to sail beyond this point!"

"Why not?" asked an amazed Julius. Luke and Aristarchus joined in the amazement. Never had they, nor anyone else, seen Paul so entrenched.

Paul raised his head, almost as if to sniff the days ahead. His voice was grave, his face drawn and pale. "The Etesian winds. They are coming. They are *here*. Never, never sail the Etesian winds."

"But they are not due for a few more days," said the captain.

"They will come *tomorrow*. And when they come, they will bring destruction. *Never* sail the Etesian winds."

"It is only forty miles," grumbled the owner of the ship, irritated at being rebuked by a prisoner.

Paul dropped his voice:

"Sirs," he said, "I believe there is trouble ahead if we go on—shipwreck, loss of cargo, injuries, and danger to our lives."

It was Julius who made the final decision. It would be the last decision that contradicted Paul's advice. The ship pulled out of the shallow harbor and struck its sail for the western end of Crete. But it would not be forty miles to the next harbor. It would not even be reached in the winter of that year. It would be spring before the passengers of that ship ever approached another harbor!

EPILOGUE

It is here, dear reader, that I, Priscilla, must leave you.

Please remember that the story I have recounted to you took place many years ago. Today, as I write, I am quite old. Many years have passed since Paul's voyage to Rome.

Today, as I close this story, they are all dead. Eleven of the original Twelve have met a violent death. Of the nine men whom Paul trained in Ephesus, all but one have died. Gaius still lives.

John Mark has died in Alexandria, Egypt, refusing to deny his Lord even as he was pulled asunder by wild horses.

Perhaps you have read Luke's account of Paul's journeys. You will also notice that Luke's story ends very abruptly. There is a reason for that. Even while he held pen to paper, Roman soldiers broke into his hiding place and carried him away to prison where he, too, eventually met his death.

Recently I have lost my dearest and most precious friend and lover, my beloved husband, Aquila. After Nero degenerated into madness, we fled Rome and returned to Ephesus. But even there my husband was hunted down and killed.

Now there are only two left who still bear witness to those

days: John, exiled upon the island of Patmos; and Gaius, who has escaped certain death again and again.

At this moment, Gaius is safe and in hiding. I have asked him to finish this story. He has written back to me and told me that he would be delighted to do so . . . that it would be an honor for him to recount what happened after Paul arrived in Rome. Gaius will tell you of Nero's monstrous acts as he sought to destroy all the Christians in Rome. Gaius will also tell you of the destruction of Jerusalem.

Gaius of Derbe is more familiar with the remnants of this story than anyone else still alive. I hope I live long enough to read what Gaius has to tell us as we come to the close of this era.

Because of our advanced age, all of us who lived this story will soon pass from the stage. John is ancient. Gaius is no longer the daring youth. I, therefore, leave it in Gaius's hands to write the final chapter to this incomparable saga.

I have asked Gaius to begin exactly where I have ended . . . Paul about to be shipwrecked on the Isle of Malta.

I close with these words: May you be as faithful to him who is your Lord as have been these gallant men.

—COMING SOON—

The
Gaius
DIARY

Gaius will tell of Paul's time in Rome, of the letters that the aged apostle wrote while there and of his death at the hands of Nero. Gaius will also tell how each of the Twelve died . . . as well as how Luke, Aquila, Epaphras, and the men whom Paul trained in Ephesus met their deaths.

You will not wish to miss the final chapter of The First-Century Diaries.

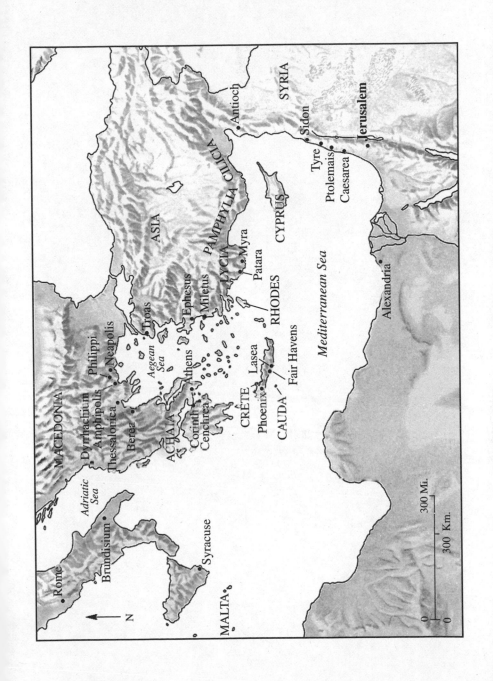

FREE!

If you would like to receive a free copy of *Revolution*, a book that covers the first seventeen years of the Christian story, you may receive one by writing to the author at

Gene Edwards' Ministry
P.O. Box 285
Sargent, GA 30275
1-800-827-9825